Howard Seely

A Nymph of the West

A Novel

Howard Seely

A Nymph of the West
A Novel

ISBN/EAN: 9783337031220

Printed in Europe, USA, Canada, Australia, Japan

Cover: Foto ©Andreas Hilbeck / pixelio.de

More available books at **www.hansebooks.com**

OF THE WEST

A NOVEL

BY

HOWARD SEELY

.

NEW YORK

D. APPLETON AND COMPANY

1888

A NYMPH OF THE WEST.

I

MIDWAY between Lampasas and San Saba, the
Colorado River runs — a wild, romantic, winding
stream. At times its placid current flows evenly over
dimpling shoals and gleaming pebbles. Again, the
waters deepen, and by flower-bordered banks its current eddies sullen, slow, and grand. But there is one
place where the river plunges madly downward to
roar at the base of precipitous rocks and writhe over
bowlders in its shallow bed. Overhead dark hem-
locks curtain this rage of waters from the gaze of
day. The sunlight enters only by stealth, and then
in tremulous pencils. At such moments, against the
somber green of the swaying pines, the red-bird
flashes, or the indigo-bird is seen—a living sapphire
in the sudden light; and the rippling melody of
rival mocking-birds enters the solemn aisles as though
the gate of heaven were left ajar. Within these aisles
the foot sinks luxuriously amid cushions of hemlock-
boughs and pine-needles; the tall, time-scarred trunks
lift themselves dimly like pillars of some leafy Gothic
dome; the vague ranks of forest exhale their cool,
damp spicery. All Nature is hushed and wan. Only
the river's moan comes faintly; and everywhere

roundabout, and pervading all things, are the twilight and seclusion beloved by the dryad.

Whether Miss Cynthia Dallas, on a certain mild
February afternoon, was at all impressed by any of
these sylvan suggestions, I can not say. Her un-
tutored mind was as yet guiltless of mythology, and
no vision of straying god or goddess, no whimsical
train of nymph and faun, had hitherto invaded her
slumbering fancy. Yet, swinging lightly in a netted
hammock, within an innermost recess of this spicy
vault, just where a slanting beam of sunlight fell full
upon her graceful figure, she might well have been
mistaken for some wood-nymph surprised amid her
favorite haunts—so quaint a figure was she, and yet
so essentially in keeping with the woodland stillness,
of which she seemed a part. She reclined at ease, and
lazily, as the hammock swung, noted the soft play of
sunlight through the boughs above, and the trembling
arabesques of spray and shadow. Her hands, holding
a small leathern whip with deer-foot handle, were
clasped behind her head, at once with graceful and
careless *abandon.* A blonde beauty, somewhat sun-
tanned and freckle-strewn, her attire a plain blue
woolen gown, that clung almost tenderly to the
charming curves of her figure ; but, swinging thus,
and with a little silver spur upon the shoe of her left
foot, tinkling as she swung, a fascinating picture, certainly, for some stumbling Strephon.

Of such amatory interruption Miss Cynthia was
happily unconscious. The dark lashes that fringed
her eyes of velvet-blue had a certain deprecatory
curve, as though they waved a playful warning against
all approaches of the tender passion. Mischief, not

sentiment, as yet dwelt behind the roguish lids. The curves of her rosy lips swept upward at the corners, where two little lines, like accents, gave her an elfish look, and mocked the sweetness of the mouth with subtle irony. And yet, so graciously had Nature touched and molded the face, so charmingly lavished upon this woodland maiden a wealth of tresses of auburn gold—tresses amid which the sun loved to linger, and glint his reckless admiration—that the impression left was at once piquant and bewitching. Possibly it was owing to this that the sun sought her out so persistently in her dim retreat, this very after-noon, thinking, with pardonable fascination, he had found his Daphne.

I must protest, however, that this fascination of Phœbus was not without its detractions. Certain locks upon the top of Miss Cynthia's head, where the golden hue had been bleached into a lighter tint, be-trayed the damaging tendencies of his caresses, as well as a reckless disregard for the bondage of head-gear. Miss Cynthia was at present bareheaded. I regret that this negligence had become a habit. There was, I believe, a felt something lying on the ground among the pine-needles, which, from the fact that it was decorated with a ribbon or two, and a gaudy wood-pecker's wing at an extravagant angle, like a sail upon the port tack, may have been once intended for a be-coming bonnet. But, at the unexpected moment of the young lady's introduction, a pet antelope fawn was attempting to browse upon it, and, from present indications, meeting with gratifying success. The antelope was assisting his prandial experiments by a vicious attack upon the hat with his sharp fore-feet.

A grave hound, seated upon his haunches at a respectful distance from this serious campaign against modern dress, regarded the antelope's sincere efforts with
a solemn approval that was certainly flattering. Cynthia, her abstracted eyes still lost in contemplation of
the swaying canopy of green above her head, or watching through a sudden vista the calm poise of a gray
hawk circling aloft in the limitless ether, was rapt
and all unconscious.

Suddenly she raised her head with a start. A
sharp, articulate cry broke the stillness. The antelope dashed away in sudden panic to a remote corner
of the bower, where he stood eying her askance—a
few feathers from the gaudy wing still clinging to
his mouth. The great hound raised himself with a
preliminary stretch and monstrous yawn, as if ex-
pecting a departure.

The girl caught up the luckless hat with a gesture
of annoyance, and a snap of her whip in the direction of the terrified fawn—a movement at which the
hound, with drooping ears and tail, was stricken into
an attitude of eloquent reproach.

"Not you, old boy," she said kindly, patting his
broad head ; "but his impudence yonder ! He knows
it, the cute rascal, and he'll hear from me later !
P'raps he thinks I'm sittin' up nights makin' lovely
hats jes' to give him a chance to try his new teeth.
Naturally not, I reckon.—But, Aulus," she continued interrogatively, addressing the grave hound,
"I'm sure I heard a noise, old boy, didn't you ?
What *was* thet ? Didn't you get to hear it ?"

The hound, raising his ears with the droll interest of dogs of that family, walked gravely to the edge

of a cliff on which the bower abutted, and looked
solemnly down. Suddenly his tail began to wag with
lively interest. The girl sprang from the hammock
with a lithe activity that left it swinging furiously
behind her. Creeping forward cautiously beside him,
she gazed below. Far, abrupt, and sheer, down the
precipitous descent, she beheld a man floundering in
the rapids. A dog, dripping wet and timorously
wretched, was following him. It was the latter
which had awakened the interest of the grave Aulus.

Both were in evident distress, and endeavoring to
effect a crossing by leaping from bowlder to bowlder
amid the whirling waters. But the rocks were slippery and moss-grown, the current dizzy and swift.
All at once the man's feet slipped on a treacherous
stone, and he tottered heavily backward. He sat
down rather than fell upon his wretched dog, who
was following him closely with frantic leaps. The
animal uttered an agonizing yelp, and with a great
splash both dog and man were precipitated into the
angry waters.

The girl threw her head back and laughed long
and musically in her sylvan bower. At the unaccus-
tomed sound a mocking-bird, that had strayed into
her retreat and perched upon a high limb, apparently
for rest and meditation, turned his pretty head to.
one side and listened attentively, as if about to favor
her with an imitation. The antelope trotted coyly
up to her. Aulus, with rapidly wagging tail and
whimpering muzzle, testified the humor of the catas-
trophe from a canine standpoint. In this sympathetic merriment Cynthia half reclined between her
pets, one arm about the hound's neck, the other

thrown caressingly around the already forgiven fawn.
The mocking-bird looked down approvingly, and
actually improvised a few bars of bubbling melody by
way of comment. Fully three minutes elapsed in
this harmonious interchange of opinion. Then the
girl crept forward again and peered below. The man
had extricated himself from the water and was seated,
chilly and miserable, upon a large rock in the middle
of the stream.

Cynthia now noticed that he carried a gun, the
barrels of which had been filled with water during his
recent immersion. He was occupied in emptying the
fowling-piece, squeezing the water from his dripping
clothing, and regarding with general discomfiture his
pitiable plight. The dog at his side, with cowering
limbs and shivering hide, was hardly less miserable
and wretched, and expressed in pathetic dumb-show
his conviction that matters could hardly be worse—
at least from a dog's limited point of view. Two
large and heavy feathered objects, which the man had
just cast down upon the rock, completed the group.

"What do you think, old boy?" said the girl,
affectionately, taking the hound by both his large
ears and gazing critically into his intelligent eyes;
"had I better help thet feller—or not?"

Aulus wagged his tail and looked interested. All
at once he raised his head, and bayed loud and deep
with a sharp recoil, as if he stood in awe of his own
vocal efforts. Apparently this was emphatic advice
that assistance was necessary. Having so delivered
himself, he was immediately overcome by a silent
melancholy, in droll contrast to his recent animation.

The girl regarded him anxiously.

"Thar! I told you so, old boy; if you will insist on exercisin' thet awful big mouth o' yours, thet bite the old badger give ye yesterday 'll never get well— never in this world, sir! Hurt you tongue, didn't it? Knew it would! My friend," she added, with a considerate gravity that was touching, stroking his great neck, "I reckon, on general principles, you better go slow with your bark."

Yet her brief colloquy with the indiscreet Aulus was evidently not without its weight. At least Cynthia acted upon it promptly. She leaned far over the cliff, holding on by the low branches of a scarred and time-beaten hemlock. A sunburst from the nodding boughs above fell full upon her red gold head and shoulders.

"Oh, stranger!"

Her voice echoed musically down the rocks. Above the noise of the rushing waters, above the tossing of the sighing pines, it reached the ear of the hapless way-farer like a silver bell. The man started and swept the sides of the ravine with a surprised and earnest glance. Suddenly his gaze became fixed. He had espied Cynthia. To the unfortunate sportsman in the gloomy chasm, the bright face peering so curiously down upon him from its coigne of vantage, was like an inspiration in the midst of his distress. His fancy transfigured her with all the graces of hope.

"Hilloa!"

The reply came clearly up to Cynthia. She put her hand to her mouth to assist her voice, and shouted down a word of homely advice:

"Throw them turkeys into the river! Don't you see thet's what's keepin' you back? Make for the

shore you've jes' left, and go down the bank a little !
I'll be down and help you over with a boat d'rectly."

Then the bright animated vignette was gone from
his fascinated eyes.   Nothing was left but the precipitous wall of the ravine, with its fringing mantle of
hemlock and pine.   As if in mockery, a fitful breeze
stirred their pliant boughs, and they bent toward him
with a grave obeisance—an ironical acknowledgment,
it seemed, of the favor they had just permitted.   It
was as though the very genius of those piny heights
had ventured to address him, and then withdrawn,
embarrassed and abashed.

The man on the rock remained for a few moments
gazing upward.   Possibly his thoughts had something
of this suggestion.   He smiled, at any rate, with a
frank good humor that threw a genial light upon
strong features, bronzed on forehead and cheek by exposure, and partially hidden beneath a light, curling
beard, more carefully trimmed than usual on the
frontier. Although begrimed and generally disordered
from his recent contact with the river's bed, there was
much about his dress to indicate the gentleman.   He
wore knee-boots, well made and of modern fashion.
His jaunty hunting-jacket had a certain cut and finish—the metal buttons being embossed with trophies
of the chase.   The hat upon his head was new and of
an excellent quality of felt.   What was more unusual,
it was becoming, and seemed in keeping with the athletic build, the manly face and bearing of the figure it
surmounted.   The gun he carried was breech-loading
and double-barreled.   A cameo ring graced the hand
that held it.   Altogether he looked the picture of a
comfortable ranchman, overtaken by embarrassing cir-

cumstances; in need of nothing so much as a warm fireside and a dash here and there of soap and water.

Such was probably his own opinion; for, after a few moments' hesitation, he acted with promptness and dispatch. He cast the two turkeys into the stream, hardly stopping to watch them as they were borne away on the rapid current, to float to some vantage-point below him. Then he looked hurriedly around a second, shivered a little, pushed his wretched dog off the rock into the water, and, quite indifferent to the pitiful yelp with which the favor was received, abruptly followed the animal. Alternately wading and leaping from rock to rock, both gained the shore —the dog immediately shaking himself and dispensing a gratuitous shower that effectually drenched his master where the river had forborne. Having thus rudely reciprocated previous kindnesses, he shrunk at once into an abject and shivering spectacle of woe, with an unconsciousness of wrong-doing, as sublime as it was dog-like.

The man recoiled, opened his mouth, as if in angry protest, abandoned the idea with grimness, and then looked wrathfully around for a stone, as more direct and persuasive in canine logic. Finding, as usual in such emergencies, that missiles were not available, and that he was confronted by bowlders and tree-trunks only, he abandoned a temporary impulse to personate Ajax, and burst into a hearty laugh. The dog, a handsome shepherd, which had meanwhile awaited dissolution with pathetic resignation, took courage at once, and thankfully wagged a dripping tail that distributed a watery benediction upon the surrounding rocks. Then he was apparently

rendered delirious by the prospect of further advance
dry-shod, and became a frolicsome nuisance, demon-
strative, unduly familiar, and generally unbearable.
The man interposed a few kicks of his heavy boot by
way of commentary upon this obtrusive pleasantry,
which was appreciated and had a salutary effect.

But here both were surprised in their diversions
by a loud call down the river—that indescribable
vocal effort which indicates a search. The man recalled himself, as if with regret for his forgetfulness,
and hurried away over the rocks along the shore,
closely followed by his gamboling dog.

II

CYNTHIA awaited the stranger. She was seated in a flat-bottomed boat at a wide bend of the river, where the water that raged above dimpled past her in sullen eddies. She had but lately rowed across, and the oars, thrown carelessly down, were beaded and dripping. With maiden recklessness, she had beached the little craft high and dry upon the rocks.

Still in no sense discomposed by the shock of landing, and entirely serene as to possible damage to the boat from the recent collision, she sat quietly in the stern, her hands crossed in her lap, but her alert eyes glancing eagerly up and down the bank in expectation. Evidently the approaching meeting had constrained her to greater formality in dress than usual, for she had donned the unfortunate hat. It now proved to be simply a soft felt, the brim of which had been caught up at one side and garnished with a ribbon or two, and the wing already mentioned. A poor substitute in feminine eyes, doubtless, for the exquisite follies of civilization, but worn amid her present surroundings with a picturesqueness and dash that were not without their charm. Beyond her the dark river, flowing with its slow but irresistible current, swept calmly on its way. The faint

green of trees upon the farther bank, the sharp outlines of rock and bowlder, framed her graceful figure
against a rugged background.   The noise of the waters above came to her ear but faintly.   High over her
head a red-shafted flicker, tapping monotonously upon
a withered limb, accented the lonely stillness of the
ravine ; while at intervals a sharp yelp of despair
drifted across the river where the abandoned Aulus,
distinctly discernible in the dim light, mounted
guard at the boat-landing and bewailed her absence.

The girl sighed regretfully.   She waved her hand
from the boat in reassurance to the faithful animal.

"Keep quiet, old man !   I'm comin' back d'rectly !" she shouted.

But her reflections were less amiable.

"I reckon thet chap allows me to be pretty ac-
commodatin', waiting to ferry him over till nigh onto
sundown.   P'raps he thinks it's my reg'lar business
rowin' half-drownded men and wet dogs across the
Colorado.   P'raps," she continued, glancing down in
the bottom of the boat where the dripping bodies of
the turkeys she had picked up on the way over were
lying—"p'raps he reckons it's pleasant entertainment
haulin' his game into the boat and gettin' soaked into
the bargain.   I wonder now, naturally, if thet's his
opinion."

But here a mournful succession of bays and howls
from the aggrieved Aulus interrupted her medita-
tions.

She sprang to her feet, impatiently seizing an oar,
as if to push the boat off and recross the river.   A
brief moment she stood thus erect, her blue eyes flashing, the indignant blood mantling her cheek, as she

placed the blade of the oar upon a neighboring rock
and threw the whole weight of her lithe body upon it.
But her efforts were futile. The unwieldy scow remained fixed and immovable. Then there was a sharp
clatter among the rocks, the underbrush upon the
bank parted suddenly, and the dilatory stranger, followed by his effusive dog, stood revealed before her
eyes. He stopped abruptly, smiled, and, dropping
the butt of his gun to the ground, leaned upon it with
both hands upon the muzzle. The dog, evidently
surprised at the sudden meeting, sat down at once
upon his haunches, and, with panting jaws, appeared
to be including in one tremendous grin the whole encounter and the afternoon's incidents.

Thus surprised, Cynthia's resolution vanished before that charming embarrassment which sometimes
overtakes her sex. She stood a moment irresolute,
surveying the easy self-possession of the man before
her; the next, the oar, with a shower of spray,
dropped awkwardly from her nervous grasp into the
stream. Reckless of the effect of this accident upon
her future rowing, she was immediately overcome with
solicitude for her personal appearance, attempted to
adjust a straggling lock of hair, and, finally, catching
up her fallen hat and setting it quickly on her head,
sat down, a very bewitching picture of confusion, and
yet not without an effort to assert herself that only
increased her discomfiture.

The man looked amused, but straightway acted
with the decision of a frontiersman. He glanced at
the floating oar. Then he stepped quickly forward,
placed his gun in the boat, and, lifting the bow clear
of the rocks by sheer strength, shoved it off into the

2

current, stepping in adroitly as he did so.   His dog, with the imitative faculty of his kind, attempted to follow suit, but, the force of the launching being considerable, only succeeded in catching one foot on the gunwale, where he hung a miserable second, until, falling in with a loud splash, he began at once to swim after the boat, with the usual whines of distress.

Strangely enough, it needed this pitiful incident to restore Cynthia to her natural composure.   With her affection for dumb animals her assurance returned. She leaned forward and glanced boldly up at the stranger.   He was standing erect, using the remaining oar as a paddle, and urging the boat swiftly in pursuit of the lost one, which, already in the sweep of the current, was drifting rapidly away.

" Don't you reckon you better haul thet poor pup in, jes' naturally ? " she inquired, fixing her critical eyes upon him.

The man glanced at her in amazement, and burst into a ringing laugh.

" Certainly, if you say so," he said, good-naturedly, arresting his oar.   " But to lift him in now means a shower-bath for both of us.   It's a neat little way with him in return for such favors," he added, with pardonable irony, in view of his recent experience. " However, I can stand it," glancing down at his dripping boots and trousers ; " but I thought you'd object, you see."

" Don't you worry about me," returned Cynthia, frankly.   " Them turkeys settled thet ! "   She paused, and whipped her bespattered skirt about her pretty ankles by way of comment.   Then, with a toss of her head, she went on :

"I reckon thet gobbler'll weigh nigh onto twenty-five pounds. I had all I could swing to. It was nip and tuck for a while whether he'd pull me in or I him, but—*I beat!*"

She laughed, and touched the great turkey with her foot, as she exulted over her exploit in girlish triumph.

Her companion, having his attention for the first time attracted to the recovery of his game in this direct fashion, thanked her warmly, and applauded her achievement. His praise was received with apparent gratification, and a sudden revelation of brilliant teeth and becoming dimples.

Meanwhile the struggling dog had overtaken the drifting boat, and was making impotent efforts to clamber in, falling back repeatedly, with agonized whining.

The girl sprang forward suddenly and caught him by the collar. She attempted to lift him in bodily, but without success. With her hand still upon the leathern strap, she turned impatiently to the stranger:

"Are you going to stand there, as if you was moonstruck, and let your poor dog drown—naturally?" she inquired.

Thus besought, the man stooped down, and, without more ado, lifted the dog into the boat, receiving at once the customary tribute. It was delivered, on the present occasion, with a frankness and devotion to detail that made it noteworthy. In addition to drenching the two in the boat, it rendered occupancy of the seats unpleasant, and boating an actual hardship.

During this animated cascade, Cynthia covered her face with her hat and shook with laughter. The man turned his back upon his dog with manifest disgust. As soon as it was safe to do so, he faced about and regarded Cynthia with grim amusement.

"He did right smart, didn't he ?" she inquired, looking up brightly at him, her eyes still dancing with her recent merriment.

"For an ordinary dog," replied her companion, quietly, "a modest, unobtrusive, unassuming brute, I should think he did. Of course, if he has any ambition of becoming a water-spout—any little ungratified longings in that direction which he may have hitherto concealed from me — I refrain from expressing an opinion."

Much of this last speech was necessarily lost upon Cynthia. Yet, while a trifle overawed by the fluency of her companion, she realized, in a general way, that it was ironical, and reciprocated his sentiments. The smile that still lingered in her roguish eyes vanished as she concealed her ignorance by an emphatic agreement.

"I reckon *so*," she said, quickly. Then, casting a sudden glance down the river—"Don't you reckon there'd be more sense in gettin' thet oar, than jes' wastin' daylight talkin' about your dog ?"

The brusqueness of this rebuke was lessened by a quiver of mirth that twitched the corners of her rosy mouth and flashed from her mischievous eyes. The man looked at her searchingly and with a grave surprise at her abruptness. Without a word he turned the boat again into the current, and began to paddle

with a rapidity that seemed an apology for his recent
negligence.

Until the oar had been recovered, and they were
rowing back against the sullen current, the silence
that had fallen between them both had been in
marked contrast to their previous merriment. This
increased so manifestly as they proceeded, that Cynthia
began to be distressed.

The sun no longer visited the river in occasional
shafts and stray glimpses. It was sinking below the
wooded heights. The afternoon was declining. A
dim twilight seemed to fall from above, and dark
shadows were gathering along the shore. A vague
chill crept over the river. The stranger shivered and
suddenly addressed her. It brought a certain relief
to Cynthia.

"Where do you live, young lady?"

The girl experienced a delicious tremor at this
form of address. His voice was low and deep, and
there was a quiet dignity about his manner.

"Up at the ranch—back of the bluff."

"Whose ranch?"

"Father's."

"And his name?"

"Dallas—Alcides Dallas, but they call him 'Al'
for short—that is, some do. But others call him
'Allsides'—Buck says it's 'cause he's uncertain in
his votin'. They can't allers count on him for the
Democratic ticket. My name's Cynthia."

Her companion, having already experienced the
divine despair of the average Republican in Texas,
was not wanting in his appreciation of the woes of
the elder Dallas. Howbeit, he made no political

comment beyond a grave lifting of the eyebrows.
But the name haunted him.

"Cynthia," he said, repeating it slowly—"Cynthia
Dallas. How do you get to your ranch, Miss Cynthia?"

"Not Miscynthia—but plain Cynthia," she said;
"or 'Cynthy,' as father says, but I hate that. *You*
can call me Cynthia."

Her companion looked up with a smile as he noted
the privilege conveyed by her emphasis.

"Thanks," he said, simply. "Well, Cynthia, do
you suppose your father has any room at his ranch
for a miserable, tired, half-drowned hunter—a 'tender-foot' we'd better call him; for he was fool enough
to let his horse walk off and leave him on the bald
prairie while he was looking up a turkey-roost?"

Cynthia's curiosity and sympathy were awakened
at once.

"Your pony walked off and left you, did he?
Well, now!" She laughed. Then, as her frontier
instincts asserted themselves, there was a little disdain in her manner as she inquired, "Can't you tie
the cow-boy's hitch?"

Her companion felt the implied slur, for he colored
visibly under his beard.

"I must have been careless, I suppose, or else the
knot slipped," he replied, apologetically. "At any
rate, that's the state of the case : no horse ; rider wet,
tired, and hungry ; dog ditto. Do you suppose your
father can give shelter for the night to two tramps?"

"I reckon," said the girl, simply. She stooped
to pat the dog's wet head compassionately. "Poor
'Ditto'!" she murmured. Then, looking up quickly

with a mischievous glance, "What's the name of the other tramp?"

"He calls himself Henry Bruce for want of a better, and he hails from the 'Mesquite Valley Ranch,' of which you may have heard," returned her companion, showing by a humorous twinkle that her sarcasm was appreciated.

"The 'Mesquite Valley Ranch!'" exclaimed Cynthia, with an astonishment of manner that she did not attempt to conceal. "Ye don't say! Well, Henry Bruce, I don't reckon you'll have any call to complain of the treatment you'll get from father. Barrin' the fact that a stray steer o' yours gets into our corn-bin now and then, he hasn't anything to complain of."

All at once her thoughts reverted to the ranchman's straying horse. Dumb animals possessed a peculiar interest for Cynthia.

"Won't that poor pony of yours get a whalin', naturally?" she inquired. "I wonder where he is now?"

"I suppose his present address is 'Texas—On the Wing,'" replied her companion, with gravity. "On general principles, yes, I think I may safely say he'll have an intelligent idea later of the capacity of a quirt. But I shall have plenty of time to consider all that, and possibly to get over my temper before I see him again. Meanwhile," he added, with a shrug of his broad shoulders, "I'm feeling a little chilly, and very much in need of dry clothing. Excuse me, Cynthia, but if you could hurry matters a little, and get me home, it would be better for all concerned."

The girl responded with promptness to this appeal.

"I reckon you're right," she said, quickly, and with a sudden blush that was very becoming. "It's mighty slack in me to be so careless, sittin' here botherin' you with questions, and you freezing to death. Hand me thet paddle."

She pointed out a small oar that had hitherto lain unperceived in the bottom of the boat.

"Now, if you'll row for all you're worth against this current, I'll have you at the landing in a jiffy. We're almost there, anyhow."

So saying, she put the paddle behind her, and, with a dexterous sweep of it, turned the boat's head to the shore. A large, flat rock in a sheltered nook, near which several stakes had been driven into the river's bed, was visible a short distance ahead. The expectant "Aulus"—a solemn sentinel in the shadow of the great bowlders that rose behind and about him —awaited them with nervous impatience. It was the landing-place.

A few strokes of oar and paddle brought them there. From the twilight of the river the boat passed with a sharp, grating sound into the gloom of the precipitous bank. Henry Bruce stepped forward with the rope in his hand and fastened it firmly. But hardly had the bow touched the rock, when the clumsy hound sprang into the scow, and, after greeting his mistress with uncouth caresses, began a jealous inspection of the stranger's dog. The result was apparently unsatisfactory, for he uttered a low growl, and the hair upon his back and neck began to bristle.

"Down, Aulus!" cried the girl, tapping him smartly with the paddle. "Aren't you ashamed of yourself, sir?"

The hound subsided, and became abject at once. Bruce had already taken a strap from his pocket, and, after securing the turkeys' legs together, thrown the heavy birds across his shoulder. He was waiting to assist her. Cynthia stooped, and quite unaffectedly handed him his gun, which he had for the moment forgotten. There was something Amazonian in the gesture. The gentleman received it with grave courtesy; then he took the plump little hand which she extended to him frankly, and she leaped lightly upon the rock, followed by her attendant dogs. It was as if Diana, the huntress, were returning from an aquatic excursion.

A steep, winding path, skirting rock and bowlder, led to the heights above. The girl at once took the lead, calling to her companion to follow her. She climbed quickly up the ascent with a practiced ease that showed her familiarity with her surroundings. The very dogs were scarcely less agile. Here and there she stopped, flushed and panting from her efforts, to regard Bruce from some superior point, and to instruct him in his future progress. Sometimes she would clasp the sweeping boughs of an adventurous cedar, and, held thus against the curtain of green overhead, smile back at him with roguish encouragement. There was something in this friendly espionage that was stimulating to the sportsman. He felt the inferiority of his sex under circumstances where it should have been triumphant. He redoubled his exertions among the slippery stones and roots, but, encumbered as he was with his gun and the heavy game, his progress was necessarily slow. At length, out of breath and quite exhausted with his hard climbing, he reached the elevated plateau. The girl was awaiting him.

As he stepped out from the dense fringe of pine and hemlock that bordered the river, the level rays of the declining sun at first dazzled him. It was like emerging from some twilight cloister into the open day. A small cotton-field, with shreds of the woolly crop still clinging to the dry and withered plants, stretched before him in dull monotony. Beyond it, amid a grove of great pecans that formed a favorable barrier against unwelcome northers, stood a small stone house, with its tall adobe chimney. Smoke was curling from the latter, bringing with it suggestions of comfort that appealed to the wayfarer. The sun was going down—a great globe of fire—behind the low hills to the west. There were the clanking of stock-bells upon the air, the bleating of sheep, and other sounds which—albeit unmelodious in themselves—are not without their compensations upon the frontier. The young man turned to Cynthia.

She was seated on a fallen tree, engaged in loosing the antelope which she had tethered to one of the branches before descending the cliff. The fawn, recognizing an addition to the party in the ranchman's dog, was timid and wary. She finally succeeded in reassuring it somewhat, and with her pet tripping daintily on before and tugging at the confining rope, proceeded. Her companion quietly took his place at her side.

"Something of a scramble, wasn't it?" Cynthia inquired, glancing at him slyly from under her drooping lashes, not without a feminine appreciation of his splendid height.

Bruce acquiesced, shifting his gun from his burdened shoulder to a more comfortable position. She regarded him a moment critically.

"You're feelin' pretty well tuckered now, ain't you?" she finally said, as the result of this inspection.

The young man met this direct query with the customary untruth of suffering manhood under similar circumstances.

"Land!" said Cynthia, waving a diminutive hand in protest; "thet climb isn't a circumstance. I can take you to a hundred worse places than thet, right here on this river."

"Not with these turkeys on my back, if *I* know it," he remonstrated.

The girl laughed at the suggestion.

They had passed through a thorny chaparral, and were close upon the ranch. The sound of a violin, playing a mournful and lugubrious air, at times bursting into sudden erratic strains, with fitful minors and jarring discords, and accompanied with violent sawing and scraping of the instrument, reached them audibly. The effect was weird and indescribable.

"Are you married?" Cynthia inquired abruptly, stopping short in the way and leveling her blue eyes full upon him with steadfast scrutiny.

The unexpectedness of this inquiry was too much for the sportsman. He threw back his head and shouted his amusement. The girl appeared relieved at the action.

"I reckon you ain't," she said at length. "You couldn't laugh like thet, I s'pose, if you were. Father says that tune he's a-playin' is 'Married Life.' *I* think it's dreadful. It's one of his own, and he says it's the result of experience. I thought, perhaps, I'd better give you warnin'. Come in now and I'll make you acquainted."

She lifted the latch of a rude gate, and together they passed into the ranch inclosure.

III.

An old man, with long, gray hair and unkempt beard, was seated on the door-stone of the ranch, playing a violin. A tall, muscular young fellow lounged against a neighboring live-oak, listening and placidly smoking. Lost in the rendering of his dismal music, the face of the performer was vacant and rapt. His eyes had an uncertain wandering gleam, and he bent his chin upon the instrument and hugged it close to him with long sweeps of his bow, as though intent upon the pursuit of some elusive melody that he feared might escape him. The nimble fingers of his left hand tracked the wandering strains up and down the key-board, and his right seemed to smite them into piteous remonstrance. His knees were pressed close together, and one foot rested on the other, the toes turned inward, with a humorous suggestion that his musical efforts were demoralizing his lower limbs. Near these erratic feet a monstrous river cat-fish, recently caught and thrown carelessly down, stretched its unwieldy length.

He did not cease playing as Cynthia and Bruce approached, but, quite unconscious of their presence, continued waking the echoes of the gathering twilight with his fiendish music. His companion greeted the girl with a friendly nod, and, quickly detaching himself from the tree, stepped toward her. The movement brought the fiddler to himself, who, still playing, turned his body half round, and as soon as his eyes rested upon the stranger, stopped abruptly, the instrument giving an impatient quaver as the bow fell away from the strings. He stared blankly at Cynthia, but said nothing.

· "Mr. Henry Bruce, father, of the 'Mesquite Valley Ranch,'" said his daughter, with a sudden blush. "He's lost his pony, fell in the river, and wants to know if you can take care of him overnight."

The old man stared again, laid down his bow and fiddle upon the door-stone, extended a heavy hand, long-fingered and big-knuckled, to Bruce, and, after closing upon the latter's fingers and lifting his arm as if it had been a pump-handle, restored both to him a trifle maimed, and without uttering a word. The same formality was then gone through with the younger individual, whom Cynthia addressed as Buck Jerrold. This gentleman managed to ejaculate "Howdy?" in a tone as mechanical as the previous gesture.

Meanwhile old Dallas had straightened out his dangerously involved legs, crossed them, and, with his hands clasped over his knees, was gazing up into his guest's face with a puzzled gravity that began to be embarrassing.

"Who be ye?" he finally said, with a doubtful look, putting his hand to his ear, as if he were listening from a remote locality. "Whar did ye say ye kem from?"

Bruce was about to reply, when Cynthia inter-

posed and repeated her previous remark more emphatically. "He's been playin', ye see ; he gets so
far over yonder thet it takes him a long time to get
back," she explained.

"Been—in—the—river—and—lost—his—horse !"
the elder Dallas finally ejaculated, slowly, as if a light
were breaking in upon him. Then he rubbed his
hands together and chuckled softly to himself, turning his head to one side, and closing his eyes, as if
there was something very amusing in the recollection.

"Wal, wal ! ef this yer State ain't gettin' swamped
with tender-foots, my name ain't Alcides ! Lost his
hoss—let it walk off and leave him !" he repeated,
chuckling again.—"Ye might build up a bustin' fire
in that thar grate, Buck, and thaw him out, I reckon," pointing to the open hearth within. "Ye kin
do that much."

Bruce, who had listened to the commentary of the
elder Dallas upon his mishap with outward impertur-
bability, but inward impatience, hereupon attempted
to say something in his own defense, when Cynthia
broke in :

"Pretty near as bad a case, father, as when old
'Jule' went off and left you down at the 'Live-oak
Water-hole,' the time you got down to doctor thet old
ewe that was snake-bit—aren't it ?" she commented,
coming bravely to the rescue.

"It's gettin' dark," said the old man, rising abruptly, and with a sudden cracking of his rheumatic
joints—"it's gettin' dark, and I reckon we better go
in." He stooped and made a feeble clutch for his re-
linquished fiddle, but his halting knees were unequal
to the effort, and Jerrold handed it to him. He

turned on the door-step, and picked a note or two
with absent eyes and a wandering hand.

"Thar ain't but two bedrooms in the house, outside the settin'-room, and them's occupied," he said,
vaguely, as if to the remote landscape, punctuating
his discourse with nervous strumming of the instrument. "Ye'll hev to 'make down' with Buck and
me on the floor, afore the fire. Ez for dry clothes,
the only extrys on hand at this ranch is a buffalo-
robe and a yaller 'slicker'—ye kin take yer ch'ice.
P'raps, ez it is, and thar being a corner in dry-goods,
outside o' woman's duds and fixins, ye better let them
clothes o' yourn dry on ye, and het up from the inside. Ye look stout, and I'll allow ye kin stand it !
—Cynthy, whar's thet rye-whisky the sheriff gin me
over at the 'barbecue' last week ? Ye might bring it
out and start your fr'eud onto it.—Buck, go to the
wood-pile and fetch an armful of wood."

So saying, and without pausing for a reply, he at
once led the way within, followed by Bruce and Cynthia. A wood-fire burned upon the ample hearth,
the leaping flames roaring and crackling up the great
chimney, and lighting up the dim interior with fan-
tastic play of light and shadow. The room was bare
and scantily furnished ; the ceiling peaked, showing
the joinings and rafters of the roof. In the center of
the rough floor stood a long wooden table, already set
for the evening meal. A few poor prints, recklessly
lavish in coloring and villainously out of drawing,
hung upon the walls. They emphasized the claims
of various events and personages upon a forgetful pos-
terity. Conspicuous among these artistic triumphs
were the "Storming of the Alamo," amid such realis-

tic detail of smoke and flame as to suggest a more
fiery locality, and a captivating portrait of General
Houston, arrayed in the picturesque glories of a red
flannel shirt. The spreading antlers of a deer graced
the broad chimney-piece, from which depended a shot-
pouch and powder-horn, one or two rawhide hopples,
a pair of large spurs, and a heavy leathern quirt.
There was a book-rack at one end of the room, between two shutterless windows, roughly fashioned out
of Southern pine, and shining red in the fire-light. It
contained a few books and papers—the scant library
of the ranch. Below it stood a little writing-stand,
rudely littered with paper, pens and ink, pistol-car-
tridges, medicine-bottles, pipes, plugs of tobacco, and
other incongruous articles heaped in amusing contrast. In the midst of this picturesque confusion
rested a little chip work-basket, from which peeped a
small blue stocking and two diminutive kid slippers,
with extravagant heels—the latest Texan rendering
of more stylish absurdities at the East. A silver-
mounted "Derringer"—also a tenant of the work-
basket—rested confidingly across these triumphs of
the shoemaker's art, and, from the singular intimacy
thus permitted with the belongings of the owner, suggested a practical turn of mind, to say the least. The
amused eyes of Henry Bruce had scarcely noted these
inconsistencies, when the work-basket was caught up
suddenly by the blushing Cynthia, and whisked with
embarrassed haste into the privacy of her adjoining
bedroom.

She soon appeared again, and sought a door at the
opposite end of the room, which gave upon the neighboring kitchen. Thence proceeded the rattle of cook-

3

ing-utensils, and a savory steam that appealed to the
fatigued and hungry sportsman.   A few minutes later
Cynthia reappeared, accompanied by an old negro
woman, turbaned and of middle age, who carried a
large black jug and a couple of glasses.   This was the
ebony "Amelia," the presiding genius of the mysterious and appetizing realm she had just quitted.

She handed a tumbler to Bruce, as he stood with
his back to the blazing hearth, exhaling a cloud of
steam in his efforts to act upon the old man's advice,
and, throwing the jug over the hollow of her elbow
by a dexterous movement of a black forefinger slipped
through the handle, stood ready to administer the
liquid refreshment.

"Say 'when,' sah !" she directed, tilting the liquor
at a rapid rate into the proffered glass.

"When !" said Bruce, hastily, glancing at Cynthia over his half-filled tumbler.

"Sho !" laughed the ebony Amelia, chuckling, and
favoring the young man with a dazzling dental display in her amusement.   " Dat ain't a 'marker' fo' a
young chap wot's jes' be'n baptized !—Heah, boss !"
—turning to old Dallas, who had been silently regarding Bruce and his protestations against her generosity
—" show this gemman wot you 'lows to be de aberage
Texas 'rejubenator.'   Dey am no sca'city ob de article !"

Alcides Dallas stole a quick glance at Cynthia, as
she sat between the two dogs dozing in a corner of
the hearthstone, with one arm around the prostrate
"Aulus," and her eyes gazing into the blazing grate.
Then he stumped eagerly forward.

" My shoulder bein' a leetle bad to-day, whar I

was throwed last spring, at the 'round-ups,' " he remarked, apologetically, his eyes still upon the silent
Cynthia, "and thet old centypede-bite of five year
ago still a-goin' fur me at times, and contributin' to
make life a weariness of the flesh, I reckon a small
snifter taken under sich depressin' sarcumstances
might operate as a blessin' in disguise."

He paused after this lengthy explanation, put his
tongue in his cheek, and looked warily around. There
was a dead silence. Mr. Buck Jerrold, who had just
entered, stooping under a heavy load of wood, cast
down his burden upon the blazing hearth, amid a
shower of sparks, and, leaning against the chimney-
piece, grinned incredulously as he listened to the old
man's catalogue of his infirmities. Cynthia sat still,
between the dogs, and said nothing.

"It's powerful sing'lar, Al," remarked Mr. Jerrold, slowly, rubbing his bearded chin and pursing
his lips, "how long it do take, natchally, to git thet
thar centypede-pizen out'n a man's unfortunet system
when wunst he's be'n bit. You don't seem to hev no
kind o' success, altho' you've be'n picklin' ye'se'f off
an' on for it nigh onto five years. Thar's Jed Smalley,
who allows thet he got outside of a clean gallon o' Jim
Wily's rat-pizen thet time he sot down on one durin'
shearin', and altho' that's ten year ago, and he's signed
the pledge sence then, he allows there's days now
when the old symptoms gets ahead o' him, and he's
obliged to hobble his conscience and take a drink, or
go clean crazy."

The old man turned, with his glass in his hand,
and gazed doubtfully at Buck Jerrold, as if to fathom
the sincerity of his remarks.

- "Thet's so," he said, gravely. "Thar's them ez believes ye never *kin* git over it! Thar's them ez thinks it's jest flyin' in the face of Providence to ever sign the pledge arter ye've once be'n bit. The train of infirmities and worryment thet an able-bodied centypede kin let loose fur evermore on an unfortunet critter's distracted inside is too harrowin' fur argymint."

But here the humor of his reflections infected even his own sepulchral gravity, and the corners of his mouth twitched; he turned his back on Cynthia, permitted Amelia to fill his glass to the brim, and then, covering it with his whole hand, so that the amount of his indulgence was concealed from his audience, tossed the draught off with surprising facility. He returned to his seat apparently refreshed.

Cynthia rose at once with a sigh, and repairing to the closet, returned with a large tablespoon and an ominous-looking bottle.

"Now, father," she said, standing before him and looking anxiously into his face, "it's time to take the 'counter-irritant.' Ef your shoulder is plaguin' you again, to-night, you want your dose. I s'pose it tastes about as bad as it smells, but it's only a minute, you know, and it's all over, and then we won't hear any more about 'sufferin' humanity' the rest of the evenin'."

She poured out a tablespoonful of the mixture and held it toward him, coaxingly.

"Go 'long, now, Cynthy!" ejaculated the old man, waving this medicinal favor aside. "Ye don't reckon I wanter mix two kinds o' medicine to onct, do yer? Thar ain't no sense in sech work ez thet! Wot I jes'

took is kalkerlated to fortify me agin the lingerin'
effects o' thet thar pizen critter's bite, and thet Injun
chollygog' hez jest the opposite effect, and would be
wearin' on the narves. No, Cynthy, I'm feelin' better
a'ready, sis, and I don't know ez I owe my inside
any partickler grudge to be depressin' it to thet extent."

He turned his back abruptly upon his daughter
and her solicitations, and, swinging round in the
wooden chair on which he sat, crossed his legs and
gazed fixedly into the blazing coals, with an expression upon his withered face from which there was no
appeal.

Thus repulsed in her efforts to counteract what
she believed to be the dangerous tendencies of liquor,
Cynthia made one more appeal.

"But you know, father, Dr. Stethyscope pre-
scribed this for you whenever you were feelin' blue
and out of spirits," she pleaded, a pretty trouble
gathering in her anxious brows.

"Dr. Stethyscope is a crank and a cussed fool!"
returned the elder Dallas, sharply, still with averted
back. "I kin run my own inside without any advice
from him, I reckon. Wot's more," he added, with a
grin that disclosed a few lonely and discolored teeth
in his upper jaw, "jest at present, *I'm not out of
sperrits.*"

He glanced at Mr. Buck Jerrold, leaning against
the chimney-piece, and winked boldly, as if to clinch
the suggestion.

Cynthia, heaving another little sigh, poured the
contents of the tablespoon back into the bottle, and
replaced it in the cupboard with an air of resignation.

She then returned to her seat in the corner of the hearth between the sleeping dogs.

Meanwhile Amelia had crossed the room to a point near the lounging Mr. Jerrold, and stood listening seriously to the dialogue between father and daughter before proffering her services to him. She now performed the same gymnastic feat with the jug, and extended the old man's empty tumbler.

"I hai'n't no use for it," replied Mr. Jerrold, listlessly, not changing his attitude, but permitting his large gray eyes to wander in the direction of Cynthia. "Never havin' be'n bit yet, and bein' favored with a right smart appetite and good works gin'rally, I kin jest natch'ally run myself satisfactory without reg'larly firin' up the machinery. Now and then, in a matter of bizness—ef a man don't come to time over a hoss-trade or swappin' cattle—when the facts don't, so to speak, keep tally with the argyments —liquor is well enough to bring conviction. It's a powerful exhorter and convincer of the jedgment. Thar's nothin' ekel to it, after you've hed a row with a feller, and altho' you've settled it, ye don't quite get back somehow inter the old groove—nothin' that goes quite so far towards puttin' things on the old familiar basis. And they tell me thet when a man's girl hez gone back on him," he added vaguely, gazing abstractedly at a point in the wall directly over Cynthia's downcast head—"when he's feelin' lost and strange like, an' the color hez jes' dropped out o' things natch'ally—they tell me thet then it's downright necessary, and the only friend you've got left. Thet's wot I hear, anyway, comin' from older men than me, and them as oughter know. One day p'raps

I may know more about it. But for ordinary daily
livin' and dyin' I don't need any in mine, and I
reckon I oughter be glad on't."

Having delivered himself to this effect, he glanced
quickly at Cynthia again, and relapsed into silence.
Amelia helped herself gravely to the contents of the
tumbler, with the remark that she hated to see "sech
good whisky lef' like dat clean out 'n de cold," and
then departed abruptly for the kitchen. Cynthia
raised her beautiful eyes to Jerrold and thanked him
for his reflections with a smile so sweet and engaging,
that Bruce, wet as he was, set down his half-filled
glass upon the mantel-shelf as quietly as possible.
Then a silence fell upon the little group—perhaps
induced by the drowsy warmth and that tendency to
reverie promoted by a blazing fire. The snoring of
the dogs, fast asleep upon the hearth-stone, was heard
distinctly in the stillness.

These reflections were broken in upon a few minutes later by Amelia, who emerged from the kitchen,
carrying a big dish of fried cat-fish and a steaming
coffee-pot which she placed at the head of the table.
Cynthia sprang up at once, and taking from the
mantel-shelf a large metal lamp, began to wind it up
with a key like a clock. She struck a match and
ignited the wick, placing the lamp in turn upon the
table. The broad, steadfast flame illuminated the
farthest corners of the bare room. The machinery
within made a loud whirring sound.

"The ole lamp makes consider'ble fuss, but she
burns ez well ez ever," said the old man, taking his
seat at the festive board without further ceremony.
"I've hed thet yer nigh onto twenty year—brought it

with me from Caroliny to the Lone Star—it was one
of my weddin' presents.   Cynthy tell Ameelyer to
hurry up with them flapjacks and potatoes.   I'm nigh
starved !—Set down, boys, and don't be hankerin'
after victuals thet's jes' gittin' cold afore yer eyes.
—Cynthy, you pour the coffee, and I'll rastle with
the fish."

With this homely introduction, he at once at-
tacked the viands.   The rest of the company cheerfully followed suit.   Throughout the informal meal
Miss Cynthia Dallas presided with her usual grace,
pouring the coffee with frontier generosity and recklessness, and serenely unconscious of the fact that
sugar and milk are indispensable to that luxury in
more civilized localities.

Later, when the appetite of the voracious Alcides
Dallas had succumbed to the abundant supply of cat-
fish and flapjacks, they all returned to the fire and
seated themeslves variously about the blazing hearth.
After a long interval of gazing at the pulsating coals,
the old man delivered himself sententiously to this
effect :

"It bein' a leetle chilly here, this evenin' "—in a
low, confidential tone, as if in confidence to the glowing embers—"it bein' a leetle chilly to-night, I allow
thet ef I axed Ameelyer to make a good pitcher o'
egg-nog, it might help matters, and obligate the mists
of adversity and depression to not so monotonously
prevail—that is, if them durned hens hev concluded
to lay at all lately.   Ye see we've made a beginnin'
on thet rye whisky," he added, by way of apology.—
"Ameelyer, wot account hev ye got to give of them
pertickler hens ? "

Amelia, who was busily engaged clearing away the remnants of the recent supper, paused at the table in the act of scraping a dish.

"Bless yo' soul, boss, de hens am all reg'lar! I've done got five eggs a day ever sence I fed 'em thet raw meat."

"I wanter know!" said the old man, in gratified surprise, without removing his eyes from the hearth, "Wal, then, you might beat up about a dozen o' them eggs in a pitcher, and empty the rest o' thet bottle on 'em to keep em from spilin'. I'm anxious not to get them pains ag'in. P'raps it won't do to keep my supper waitin' too long for it."

"De Lor'!" exclaimed Amelia, rolling her eyes in amazement; "yo' doan' wan' de hole bottle o' whisky in dem eggs, boss! Do yo' wan' cook em into one paste same as an om'lette? One teaspoonful to ebery egg, sah—dat am de correc' proportion."

"Wal, let her go at thet, then!" sighed the old man, querulously; "so long ez you don't give thet centypede time to get to work on my inside afore yer on hand with it."

Amelia disappeared in the kitchen forthwith, and soon returned with the coveted beverage in an earthen pitcher. The glasses were filled and set round.

"Thet's a right peart shootin'-iron o' your'n, Mr. Bruce!" said the old man, picking up the latter's gun as it stood in a corner of the hearth-stone, and curiously examining it. "How do you load her though, without any ramrod?"

"In this way," Bruce explained, taking it from him and touching the lever, as he rested the butt against his hip. "It's a Colt gun, top-action." As he spoke, the barrel fell by its own weight, disclosing the yawning breech."

"Jeewhittaker!" exclaimed Alcides, opening his eyes. "It works like a rifle, don't it?—Wal, now, that lays way over the 'Silent Mary,' Buck, you bet. —Cynthy, bring 'Mary' out! She's standin' in the corner. I loaded her to-day, darter," he added, in a low tone of voice, as if thinking aloud, "with a handful o' salt, in case that blasted Capting Foraker comes callin' on ye ag'in durin' the next fortnight. I hain't no other use for him, and I reckon he knows it!"

Cynthia made no reply to this remark of Alcides, but soon returned to the hearth, carrying with difficulty an enormous muzzle-loading shot-gun. It was double barrelled, and evidently designed for killing geese at long range.

"I call her the 'Silent Mary,'" said the old man, setting the unwieldy weapon between his knees, and regarding it admiringly, "out of a feelin' of gentle sarcasm. She's about the loudest in argyment of any shootin'-iron I ever see. And what she hez to say, gen'rally strikes home — *sometimes both ways.* I reckoned the drum of my ear, one time, was plumb busted! But lookin' at her by and large," he added, tapping the barrel, and surveying the great gun, "'Mary' hez more p'ints and more 'git thar' than anythin' I ever yet p'inted into a flock o' geese or wild-duck."

He turned his head slowly and regarded Bruce.

"I dare say," the latter replied, considerately, "you can count on that gun for very long range, but I find mine very convenient for ordinary shooting. Won't you try a cigar?"

He opened a leather cigar-case and held it toward him. The old man took one as a matter of course, but pursued his reflections. Bruce extended the case to Jerrold, and then, lighting one himself, blew a cloud into the open fire-place.

"I don't allow thet you'll believe me," said old Dallas, biting off the whole lower end of the weed before fitting it carefully between his scant teeth, "but I hev killed geese with 'Mary' ez far as a hundred and fifty yards. I'd like to git a 'bead' with her on them fellers ez stole 'Old Spike' and them running hogs o' our'n, Buck," he broke out suddenly.

Mr. Buck Jerrold assented grimly, laying a significant hand on a revolver he wore in his belt, and tilting his cigar in his mouth reflectively.

"Are you meeting with any loss in that way?" inquired Bruce, quietly glancing at both. "I've had a little trouble of that kind myself lately."

"Ya-as," drawled the old man, "there's allus suthin' goin' wrong with yer live-stock. Ef it ain't cows, it's hosses, and ef it ain't hosses, it's hogs. Them black-and-white hogs o' mine are runnin' free, to be sure, but they've got a good road-brand, and there ain't no excuse fur huntin' 'em. But they's pork with my brand, fur sale down at San Marcus, all the same. I reckon it's Lem Wickson and his gang. I've sent word to the sheriff, and he'll be over here some day to talk it over. I perpose to hev the law on 'em.

"Dad-burn the luck!" he broke out suddenly, as recent disasters increased his impatience. "There's them fine-wooled Vermont bucks out in the pen. One on 'em didn't come to time yesterday at sundown. Found him lyin' stiff and cold in the mornin'

—pizened on laurel, I reckon ! It's enough to gravel
the patience of Job, durned ef it ain't !"

"I suppose wolves, coyotes, never attack a buck ?"
hazarded Bruce.

"Not much !" returned Alcides; "that is, not
when they're together. A coyote's knowin'. Them
bucks stand by one another, and a coyote wolf isn't
goin' to risk gettin' knocked into the middle of next
week fur a mouthful of tough mutton. A starvin'
coyote might pull one down, ef he caught him alone,
but they ain't no idea of bein' busted when their attention is otherwise engaged."

He leaned back in his chair, chuckling to himself,
and took a long sip of the egg-nog in his tumbler
with evident zest. All at once the air without was
filled with cries, as if all Bedlam were let loose—
shrieks, barks, and yells that, from their number and
frequency, might have proceeded from fifty throats.

"Speak of the devil—there they go ag'in, them
durned coyotes !" ejaculated the old man, turning
his ear to listen. "I reckon they're wranglin' over
the carcass o' thet poor old buck. I've a notion to
hump myself and let ' Mary ' off into 'em, jes' to make
'em scatter."

"Don't waste yer powder, Al—what's the use ?"
remonstrated Mr. Buck Jerrold, lazily stretching his
sturdy limbs before the fire. "It must be gittin'
along toward nine o'clock ; them coyotes is good as a
watch every three hours. Ye kin count on 'em jes'
so often—at sundown, nine o'clock, midnight, three
in the morning, and about sun-up. I wonder, now,
why thet is ?"

"Give it up !" said the old man, shortly. "Prob'ly

because the durn critters hev got jes' so much cussedness bottled up inter 'em, and they must let her off
jes' so often, or bust the safety-valve.   And one on
'em makes ez much noise ez twenty.   I never hear
one o' them devils tune up," he continued, slowly,
" but wot I think o' my wife, ez was onct, an' how
she could 'hold the fort' ef any one give her a reasonable opportunity.   I'd back her ag'in anythin' I
ever seen yet.   Thar was times in my fam'ly," he
added, sinking his voice almost to a whisper, "when
I fust come to Texas, and started in the hotel business, and the frontier not, so to speak, exactly jibein'
with Marier's eccentricities—thar was times in my
fam'ly when nothin' short of a menagerie at feedin'-
time could ekel it.   I useter sit by, them times, tryin' to console myself with the idea thet I hed the big-
gest domestic circus in the Lone Star country.   Thar
wan't much comfort in thet, somehow.   But *I'm*
here yet," he concluded, triumphantly.   " Marier
ain't, though !" he added, after a pause.

"Is your wife dead, sir?" inquired Bruce, with
all the gravity he could assume.   Cynthia glanced up
at him with a pained look.

"Don't git Al started on married life—don't,
natchally !" interposed Jerrold, hastily, with a warning gesture.

But the train was already fired.

"Dead !" exclaimed Alcides Dallas, "thet's wot
I'd like to know.   Mattermony," he further remarked,
deliberately stretching out his cramped legs, burying
his hands deep in the pockets of his ducking-trousers
and gazing dejectedly before him with bent head, as
if consulting an unhallowed past—" mattermony is a

lottery, my friend, whar there's more blanks than
prizes, and, understand me, I'm capable o' jedgin',
fur I lived with Marier nigh onto ten years, and
hevin' graduated—not with high honors—but all the
same, hevin' graduated, I'm tol'ble well up on the
subjec'. It's jes' ez I say to Cynthy here; she's a
good little girl, though, and don't gin'rally give me
any trouble on thet score—not to say thet I wouldn't
be glad to see Cynthy hitched in double harness, purvided her pardner was an honest sort o' hoss, war-
ranted sound and kind, and not likely to *kick in the
traces;* but thar's allus thet risk, and nothin's more
uncertain than marryin', I allow, unless it be swappin' hosses. My old granny useter say to my sisters—
and God knows why I didn't profit by it—I heard it
all my life : 'Gals, don't be in a hurry; fur, ef you
git a good husband, you'll be well paid fur waitin',
and, ef you make a mistake, you'll hev plenty long
enough to live with him.' I kin only repeat the
same thing to Cynthy, and hope she'll hev more sense
than I hed on the subjec'. Still, Cynthy knows wot
I think a'ready."

He paused, and glanced significantly at Mr. Buck
Jerrold, who pulled his hat-brim over his eyes, as if
to shade them from the glare of the fire. Cynthia
moved uneasily in her corner, blushed crimson, and
stole a glance at Bruce from under her drooping
lashes.

The old man drained his tumbler to the dregs, set
it down on the table with emphasis, and proceeded :

"Still, all this ain't nuther here nor there. I
kem to Texas, arter the war, from Caroliny. Marier
and I hed got along pretty well back in the States ;

fit occasionally, ye know, but thet's expected arter
the fust two years. Things was flat in Caroliny. I
'lowed to git out whar the kentry was new; sold out,
tuck Cynthy—she was only a baby then—and Marier
—I might better hev left *her*, but I didn't know enough
—and kem to Texas and started into the hotel bizness. I done well 'nuff at fust, and made money.
My house was full all the while of sheep- and cattle-
men—good pay and plenty of it. But, bimeby, arter
the novelty wore off, Marier allowed thet the kentry
didn't quite kem up to her expectations, and begun
takin' an inventory of the guests stoppin' at the house
ter alleviate her grief at the fact. The fust feller
thet she seemed to find kalkerlated to overcome the
monotony of the frontier was this here Capting Foraker I loaded 'Mary' fur this arternoon. She met
him at a 'barbecue,' and run with him consid'rable
fur a spell. Of course, I had suthin' to say on that
subjec', and arter a while this Foraker—he quit callin'!
It might hev bin bekase I was right smart at makin'
warts on silver dollars throwed up in the air, them
days, but I don't discuss that subjec'. Then thar
was a sewin'-masheen agent who presented Marier
with a masheen, and thereby, savin' Marier consider-
'ble sewin' at nights, give her an opportunity of showin' her gratitude by playin' the piany fur him onneces-
sarily in the parlor. About the same time my mend-
in' began to be uncertain and permiskiss, and the
fam'ly menagerie was on daily exhibition. The agent
fin'ly went East, and Marier languished for a while,
but one day a julery-drummer kem through—a slick
chap, with plenty o' samples o' pinchbeck and gew-
gaws. Her spirits rose ag'in, and never faltered from

thet time forward. They rose so high this time thet
she left town with that feller, one night, and I ain't
laid eyes on her sence. Marier never done things by
halves, and I never could quite onderstand why it was
she left Cynthy here behind, but it was a fortunate
thing for me she did, or I reckon I'd settled my account with a six-shooter during the next fortnight.
Not but wot I'd been willin' to settle hers fust tho',"
he added, significantly. "I'd preferred to have left
this world with suthin' to my credit. Arter that I
quit the hotel bizness and kem here ; I lent money on
live-stock, and did pretty well. Buck, here, and me
own right smart o' cattle together, and he looks arter
'em, bein' foreman o' Judge Reynolds's ranch, and
spryer and younger. I ain't heard of Mrs. Dallas
sence, and now I don't wanter.

"It's gettin' late," he said, abruptly, "and I
reckon we better make down."

He rose with a yawn and an impatient kick at the
dying embers. Cynthia rose, too, and, calling the
dogs, put them out of doors for the night ; after
which she dropped the gentlemen a quaint courtesy,
and retired to her bedroom.

The old man went to a closet, from which he took
three gray blankets and threw them down on the floor.
"One apiece," he said, with primitive hospitality,
drawing off his boots, and wrapping his ducking-coat
around them to serve for a pillow. He rolled himself
in his blanket, his feet toward the fire, and was soon
asleep and snoring audibly. Nothing was left but for
Bruce and Jerrold to follow suit. This they accordingly did.

But toward morning they were aroused by Alcides's

rising impatiently and stumping noisily to the door.
A few minutes elapsed and there was a fearful explo-
sion, the bare room lighting up with the red flash.
Bruce sat up at once, rubbing his sleepy eyes, and
inquiring the cause of the disturbance. Even in his
confused alarm he heard Cynthia laughing to herself
in her little bedroom.

"It's nothin' but cows," said Mr. Buck Jerrold,
turning over with a yawn in his blanket. "The
old man left a pair of good breeches out on the fence
to dry this evenin', and I reckon them salt-starved
cattle hev been chawin' onto 'em in the course o' their
pryin' 'round. He's seen fit to turn loose onto *them*
the load which he said he give 'Mary' this arternoon,
on account o' Foraker. It's a way of *saltin'* 'em that's
quite pop'lar here at the ranch."

IV

DAWN came, lacing with rose and amber the severing east, with purple billows breaking upon the horizon's bar, and flecking the orient with crimson and opal dyes. With the first rays of light, the cries of wild-geese were heard flying in long harrow toward the river, and the faint clang of mallard and shell-drake passing overhead. The sounds awoke Bruce, who rose cramped and stiff, and, rubbing his sleepy eyes, leaned against the chimney-piece in lazy admiration of the pageantry of early morning, seen through the shutterless windows of the ranch.

He glanced down at the tumbled heap of blankets at his feet. Only one of his companion bedfellows met his eye. Mr. Buck Jerrold had already arisen, leaving his disordered inwrappings in a tangled coil, very much as a snake casts its skin. The old man, his hands folded upon his breast, lay flat upon his back, snoring dismally in nasal derision of early rising.

Bruce regarded him a moment with an amused smile, and then, true to the sportsman's instinct, drew on his shooting-jacket, caught up his gun from the corner of the hearth, and stepped out into the cool, clear air.

He was immediately overwhelmed by the fawning

dogs. Having been making a night of it, they were seemingly desirous of testifying by their joyous welcome the general unprofitableness of nocturnal dissipation. He stooped to caress them.

As he did so, he beheld Mr. Buck Jerrold saddling his roan cow-pony, and evidently making preparations for an early departure.

"Where away at this hour of the morning?" he inquired, sauntering up.

"Back to the ranch. I've got more'n fifty young lambs to look after, I reckon."

"You're not going off before breakfast?" Bruce inquired, leaning on the gate.

"I reckon so; I don't call ten miles afore breakfast any great shakes."

"That depends on the rider," Bruce replied, pleasantly. "I don't think any one could hire me to ride ten miles this morning without a cup of coffee, at least. I feel as lame and stiff as if I'd been dragged at the end of a lariat through a thick chaparral."

"Oh, I've hed my coffee, you can bet yer life!" Jerrold replied. "Amelia's up already; she ain't the woman to let a man start out without suthin' under his jacket. I say, pardner, ef you're in any great hurry to get back to the 'Mesquite Valley,' bein' ez you're turned foot-loose and without a nag to ride on, ye can hev 'Buckshot' here fer twenty-five dollars," indicating his roan. "He ain't handsome, but he's good for twice thet distance, ez smart ez ye want to june him; he's fast and sure-footed both, and don't 'buck' nuther. Ye needn't keep yer friends waitin' and anxious. I kin rope one o' the old man's 'kaveyard' and get off easy with half an hour's delay."

He paused, bringing the much-lauded "Buck-shot" smartly around by a blow of his quirt as he did so, at the same time stooping and tightening the flank-girth.

"Buckshot," a large, raw-boned, spotted horse, with vicious eyes and Roman nose, laid his ears back in protest; then he sprang clear of the ground, with back arched like a cat, and rigid legs, striking the earth at every bound as if there were no such property known to matter as elasticity. He varied this unique performance at intervals by a plunging movement fore and aft, like a stout ship in a heavy sea. The result was soon obvious. Amid a whirling vortex of blinding dust and flying hoofs, the saddle began to turn. When "Buckshot" suspended his exertions a few minutes later, and struck a snorting and indignant tableau, with fiery eyes and flaring nostrils, the saddle was upside down, and hanging loosely between his four feet.

"No!" said Bruce, quietly, vaulting lightly over the fence, after witnessing this interesting performance; "I see now plainly that 'Buckshot' does not 'buck.' He is only a little opposed to your 'cinch-ing' the flank-girth. But I think I shall get along here very well, Mr. Jerrold, until my partner, Phil Kernochan, looks me up or something favorable happens. He knew that my general direction was the Colorado River, and that I was out after turkeys. Meanwhile the hunting is good, and I think I'll shoot a brace of mallards before the family are stirring. *Adios!* Drop in and see us the next time you're over our way. There they come now!" he exclaimed, shoving a couple of shells into his gun as he marked a small flock of duck coming down the wind. "*Adios!*"

So saying, he turned his back upon the discomfited horse-trader, and Mr. Buck Jerrold sprang at once into the saddle. Before he was fairly seated, the vicious "Buckshot" essayed to repeat his previous exploit, but he reckoned without his host.

Mr. Jerrold had improved the interval to lash a small stick back of the pommel, and now, supported on either thigh as in a vise, drove his cruel spurs into the flanks of the horse at every bound, and ruthlessly applied the heavy quirt.

"Everythin's fair in a hoss-trade," he shouted, apparently enjoying the animal's gymnastics. "I swapped this critter yestiddy for a pair of leather leggin's and a hoss-hair lariat to boot. The hoss I got rid of, tho', hed the 'lampers,' an' was dog poor at thet. The fust time the other feller attempts to put him on grain, he'll find he's got a losin' contract."

He clapped his spurs again into the discomfited "Buckshot," and, wheeling him sharply around by a jerk on the bridle, was off like a thunder-bolt.

Bruce was already far away in pursuit of the flying mallard. He had marked them down in a long water-hole, bordered by low bushes. As he crept up to the edge of the pool he caught a glimpse of the old "green-head" drake, a startled silhouette against the misty bank, with neck outstretched and eye alert. His glossy mates swung silently upon the silver mirror of the pool in the morning's gray. In an instant the wary bird was up and away, but Bruce stopped him with his right barrel, and he fell with a heavy plump upon the farther bank, his red legs straddling awkwardly as he came down. The next moment the air was full of flying teal, rising with frightened clamor and whirring away to the left. Bruce let the other mallard go, and gave the teal his left barrel, thinking of Cynthia and her damaged bonnet. Three dropped to his shot. He picked up his game hurriedly, not without a little inward exultation. There was one drake among the teal. The bright little fellow fairly gleamed in brown and emerald—his head a banded flash of color, his wings a fluttering revelation.

Bruce stood still a moment, regarding admiringly the beauties of the dying bird. A light film was settling on the flashing eye. He could not help thinking what an improvement he might make in Cynthia's appearance, were he possessed of the taxidermist's skill. With masculine self-confidence, he aspired for the moment to become her milliner.

"Ain't he a daisy?" said a musical voice.

He turned in surprise. Cynthia stood before him —a blushing Aurora, the roses of the dawn in her dimpled cheeks, the amber of the sunrise in her golden hair. With the occasional recklessness of her sex, she had arrayed herself more with an eye to picturesque effect than common prudence. She recognized the fact that there was an observer upon the scene of action more appreciative than usual. Under the circumstances, her defiance of season and climate had a touch of sublimity. She had donned a pale-blue muslin dress, exquisitely becoming, I grant, but a relic of the previous summer and a much higher thermometer. The hat on her head was of straw,

and supported a whole parterre of roses and a long,
curling feather; and she had on the high-heeled
French slippers.   They were quite wet through, and
the embroidered stockings, which a charming sense
of consistency in dress had impelled her to wear, were
beaded and flashing with dew.

Immediately after addressing Bruce, she glanced
down at her feet with some solicitude, her light
skirts gathered daintily in her left hand.   She frowned
at the slippers, already turning purple at the
toes.

"I reckon I've spoiled 'em the first time I put
'em on," she said.   "However, there's lots more
where they came from!" tossing her head with the
general suggestion that French slippers are a gratuitous donation from obliging shoemakers to the fair
sex—an attitude quite carefully preserved by womankind toward eligible bachelors, along with a becoming
disregard of the necessity of capital.   "Is thet green
wing for me, Mr. Bruce?" she inquired, with a
politeness of manner which seemed quite as unsea-
sonable, in her own case, as her faultless attire, and
in a sense to have been assumed with the gorgeous
hat.   She glanced eagerly at Bruce, as he stood sepa-
rating the bright pinion from the duck's body, and
flashing the gleaming plumes in the sunlight.   "Oh!
what a lovely little duck—a bantam!" she exclaimed,
with a sudden feminine intuition of ornithology.
"Isn't he cute?"   Then her eye fell upon a blood-
spot on the breast, and she looked suddenly grave.
"Do you reckon it hurt him much to kill him?"
she pleaded.

"Not any more than was strictly necessary under

the circumstances," Bruce replied, with the sportsman's indifference. "Good-morning, Miss Cynthia.
Yes, the green wing is intended for you, but I hardly
expected to see you at so early an hour. You look
like Aurora, I assure you."

"Like *a roarer!*" queried Cynthia, knitting her
brows in puzzled surprise. "Well, now, thet *is* a
compliment—before breakfast, too! And I haven't
said hardly a word yet. I should think I was 'Aulus.'
Did ye hear him bay when I first came out this morning?"

"No," replied Bruce, "I must have been intent
on the mallard." He held up the bright-plumaged
bird by one leg as he spoke. "But I understand how
'Aulus' felt, I think. He's not in the habit of meeting a goddess before breakfast. It disturbs the calm
equipoise of his mind."

Cynthia glanced at him in embarrassment, yet not
without a certain admiration.

"Dear me!" she sighed, "you're so dre'dful high-
toned, it most makes my head ache to see what you're
drivin' at. If you're goin' to talk to me, Mr. Bruce,
you must cut some of those words, or it'll interfere
with our gettin' acquainted."

She looked up at him in bewitching perplexity.
The level rays of the rising sun shone full in her eyes,
and she drew down her hat-brim with an impatient,
dimpled hand as she did so.

Thus besought in reference to his mythological
quotations, Bruce made haste to explain briefly to
Cynthia the fable of Aurora and Tithonus. She listened with amused surprise. When he had finished,
with the lamentable old age that overtook that unfor-

tunate lady's husband, she sighed, and expressed herself :

"So he turned out to be a grasshopper in the end
—eh ? Thet was pleasant ! Served her right, though,
for wantin' him to live forever. A girl oughtn't to
get gone on any man to thet extent—forever is an
awful long trip ! A grasshopper ! Mebbe thet's what
father means when he says matter'mony has so much
to do with 'kickin' ? '" She glanced inquiringly up
at Bruce. The latter laughed outright at this commentary. At once she turned her back on him and
regarded the sunrise.

"So you think I look like thet, do you ?" she
said, after a pause, turning to him with a sudden
gratification of manner, and pointing with a rosy
forefinger to where the tints of dawn were being rapidly lost in the splendor of the coming day.

Bruce nodded.

She walked on a few minutes in silence, with gathered skirts and a coy scrutiny of his face from under
her drooping lashes. A pleased smile lingered on her
face.

"How is it that you happen to be out to see the
truth of the comparison ?" the young man inquired.

"Oh, I had to turn the bucks out !" she replied.
"I usually do. I started 'em up the valley, and then
I heard you shoot, and thought I'd come out and see
what you'd got."

No one would have dreamed from her manner that
her motive was aught but curiosity. But there was
the testimony of the elaborate toilet, and young men
are, perhaps, more discerning than the enemy imagine.
The homage of beauty is always flattering. Bruce

was conscious of rising a trifle in his own estimation
as they fared on together.

"Dear me!" said Cynthia, sweeping the horizon
with eyes dazzled by the sun. "Where can those old
bucks have gone to? Could anything have stampeded
'em?"

A sudden succession of dull crashes, as of heavy
bodies in rapid collision, caught her ear. She turned
quickly and looked back. They had passed the venerable patriarchs of the flock — their grayish-black
bodies scarcely discernible against the withered prairie-
grass. A difference of opinion had evidently arisen
as to whether the best opportunities for pasturage lay
up or down the river. With the predilections of their
kind for forcible logic, they proposed to settle this
question by a reverberating cannonade against one
another's skulls. When Cynthia first espied them,
hostilities were in full progress, the horned combat-
ants backing off a few paces and coming together with
the shock of a tourney. Their impetuous recoils at
times threw the bewildered animals back upon their
haunches, but they staggered to their feet with a
courage worthy of a better cause, and returned in-
domitably to the charge. "Aulus," seated gravely
upon his haunches, overlooked this revival of ancient
chivalry with the gravity of a referee.

"Goodness gracious!" exclaimed Cynthia, wring-
ing her little hands in agitation; "they'll be more
funerals among the bucks if thet keeps up!"

She caught up a dry branch of mesquite at her
feet and ran fearlessly in among them. A few blows
of the thorny stick full in the faces of the charging
sheep dispelled their preoccupation. They reeled

backward, and regarded her with lifted heads and
panting nostrils. Then, with the sudden decision of
their species, they turned sharply about and moved
stolidly off in a dusky herd, as if nothing had ever
occurred to disturb their fleecy serenity.

Only one venerable pugilist remained to contest
the field with Cynthia. He had been arrested in the
fury of his onset by the discovery that his adversary
had turned tail and beaten a hasty retreat before the
blows of the demoralizing mesquite. He now stood
stamping his feet violently, and debating whether it
would not be as well to do battle with the indignant
girl. The rapid evolutions of the brandished limb at
last decided him, and he wheeled about as if to join
his comrades. At this moment he caught sight of
"Aulus," serene, unconscious, and contemplative.
Quick as a flash he lowered his head, and plunged blind-
ly forward. In vain Cynthia shouted and struck impatiently at him as he charged past her. In vain
"Aulus," catching a startled glimpse of him, strove to
swerve his unwieldy body out of the line of assault.
The leveled front of his adversary struck him full
upon his ponderous shoulder with the force of a
catapult, and, with a pitiful yelp and loss of dignity,
the sedate hound described a bewildered parabola,
ending in a succession of somersaults, chiefly remarkable for flapping ears. The ram, stopping in full
career, did not pause to survey the consequences of his
artillery, but ignominiously fled as if in dread of the
wrath to come.

Words can not describe the indignation of Cynthia. She ran after the fleeing buck until she lost
a slipper, when she was perforce obliged to abandon

the chase, and hop slowly back in search of the
missing buskin. She was met by Bruce, who had already recovered it. She put one hand upon his arm
while she readjusted the high-heeled absurdity. Then
she sought the unfortunate hound. He, too, came
forward to meet her, but with a disorganized gait and
with his right foot raised appealingly. She knelt
down and examined the damaged shoulder anxiously
with pitying murmurs of distress.

"Three days, shut up in the house on a light diet,
and Dr. Tobias's liniment," she finally said, with the
air of a veterinary surgeon. "Aulus" gave a yelp of
despair as if he understood the gravity of his affliction.
"Between badgers and old 'Fagin,' my friend, I
reckon there won't be much left of you naturally, if
this carelessness of yours continues! Do you know, I
think 'Aulus' is in love?" she said, suddenly, looking up into the face of Bruce. "It's either love or old
age, I'm blessed if I know which! He's allers sittin'
round lately, sorter dreamin', and the last week he
hasn't eaten anythin' to speak of. Father says thet's
the way it begins, and I'm not certain but thet's
what's the matter. But mebbe he's only keepin'
Lent," she added, with a mischievous glance, as she
saw Bruce laughing. "I see by the weekly paper it's
early this year, and p'raps, after all, he's an Episco-
palian—though I'd set him down along back, on
account of his bathin' so much, for an out-and-out
Baptist."

She sprang lightly to her feet, and, with cries of
encouragement to the crippled hound, accompanied
Bruce back to the ranch.

Alcides Dallas had arisen in their absence, and sat

upon the door-stone awaiting them, in a' *negliyé* so startling and characteristic, as to impress the young ranchman that attention to details in matters of the toilet was certainly not a family trait. He was without coat and hat, and his stockinged feet showed that his rawhide boots were probably still performing the office of his pillow. His long, gray locks straggled over his face, and he was fiendishly occupied with his violin. His performance was of the usual dolorous character.

"Is there any particular name for that tune?" inquired Bruce of Cynthia, as the jarring discords seemed to insult the tranquil serenity of the early morning.

Cynthia turned her head a moment and listened attentively. She might have been a mocking-bird, so characteristic was the action.

"I clean forget," she said, finally, "whether father calls thet the 'Husband's Lament' or the 'Texan Honeymoon,' but it don't make much difference which. Father's playin' is pretty much alike, and, if ye remember thet his tunes all have somethin' to do with marryin', you can't be very far wrong, no matter what you call 'em. I reckon mother didn't give him very much variety in her housekeepin', for it's had an awful monotonous effect on his music. Don't speak to him now, Mr. Bruce. He's allus easier in his mind if ye let him play a tune through; to stop him short in the middle is harrowin' to his feelin's and gen'rally crops out arterwards. Come in right away and have breakfast."

And, without a word to her sire, she piloted the amused Bruce past the absorbed violinist, leaving him still fiddling violently upon the door-step. The crippled "Aulus" stopped at the door to lift his nose to the sky and utter a long-drawn, agonizing howl of protest—with which canine commentary upon the unmelodiousness of the old man's music, he, too, abandoned him and hobbled within.

The day had worn away into the early afternoon. The northward shadows of the live-oaks were swinging gradually to the east. Far up the valley the dusky bodies of the buck-herd were seen slowly grazing toward the ranch. It was just after dinner, and the wintry sunlight on the southern wall of the ranch beat softly down with a grateful and cheering warmth. The air was slumberous and still—not a breath or a sound to break the prairie stillness, save where an occasional marmot raised his peevish bark against the oppressive silence, and disappeared in his burrow with a gurgling murmur of disapprobation. High overhead the ever-watchful buzzards were circling lazily, the sunlight flashing now and then on their gory heads as they wheeled with wings aslant.

In the sunniest angle of the ranch Bruce and his white-haired host were seated, smoking. The old man, enjoying the aroma of one of the ranchman's cigars, which he mumbled at a very precarious angle between his scant teeth, was in an expectant frame of mind and unusually genial. Cynthia was seated beneath a live-oak, playing with her fawn.

"Do you reckon them folks o' your'n 'll be anyways anxious about ye?" old Dallas inquired, blowing out a cloud of smoke, as if the chief luxury in smoking was expelling it forcibly.

"I hardly think so," Bruce replied, lazily tilting

his chair against the side of the house, with his hands clasped behind his head. He had thrown his hat on the ground, and the whiteness of his forehead contrasted with the bronzed hue of his cheeks and the luxuriance of his square, curling beard. "My partner, Kernochan, understands me pretty well by this time, and knows I generally come out all right, so he won't give himself any uneasiness. There may be a little fuss when my horse turns up at the ranch, though. I shouldn't be surprised if Phil rode over here to-morrow."

"Wal, you're takin' it pretty easy here, seein' ez they hain't the least idea whar ye be," returned Alcides, frankly. "But that's what we want to hev ye do, tho'," he added, after a pause, fearing his meaning might be misconstrued. "Visitors with agreeable manners, and good terbacker, is all-fired sca'ce in this country," he continued, with the general air of paying a compliment.

He rose from his chair with an effort due to rheumatism and the uncompromising character of his knee-joints, and swept the horizon with an anxious eye.

"Durn my skin, ef thar ain't the sheriff, after all!" he exclaimed, as a small man, mounted on a sorrel horse, rode up to the gate at a fox-trot, and, throwing himself from the saddle with a nervous impatience, proceeded to tether the animal by the lariat which hung from the pommel. His nimble fingers were quick at the task. He came toward them with a rapid step, his revolvers swinging in their holsters, and his spurs clinking as he strode.

"Wal, Ike Mosely, ye've got over here at last, hev

ye ? " said Alcides, stumping forward eagerly to meet
the new-comer. "I've been a-worryin' about this
killin' o' my stock. I reckon ye'll beleeve me, when
I tell ye I'm right glad to see ye."

"Ain't long to stay nuther," returned the sheriff,
grasping the proffered hand of old Dallas with a hurried shake, and dropping it again immediately. "I
never struck sech a rush o' bizness sence them tem-
p'rance idgits tried to ruin Texas by inauguratin' the
Brady City crusade. Ye heard about the 'Temperance Ball.' Wal, the reaction after thet nonsense
pretty near used up Ike Mosely ! I slept with my six-
shooters on me, and lived on rye-whisky, for the best
part o' six months. I don't propose to give the citizens o' the Lone Star an opportunity to lay back for
future cussedness ag'in, ef I have anythin' to say about
it. It's mos' too wearin' on the narves. Ez it is, I've
hed two hangin's already this week—to say nothin' o'
these rumors o' yours about hoss-stealin' and hog-
killin'. And now, jes' ez I was jumpin' in the saddle
to ride over here, I got word thet the road agints have
begun ag'in between Lampasas and Belton. Thet
means all I kin swing to for four weeks certain. Ef
things go on at this rate, they'll hev Ike Mosely's
hide by the time o' the spring round-ups.

"But it's mighty dry talkin'," he said, abruptly,
glancing at Dallas with a significant eye ; "an' I've
come all the way from San Marcus to look into this
yer bizness o' your'n. How did thet liquor I recom-
mended to ye turn out ?"

"I reckon it's pretty near all turned out," replied
Alcides, ruefully, somewhat discomfited by the urgent
business manner of the sheriff.—"Ameelyer !" he

called, " bring out what's left in thet thar bottle, and
a glass for Mr. Mosely.—Ike, this is Mr. Bruce, of the
' Mesquite Valley Ranch,' stopping with us for a
spell," he concluded, with a grave look, intended to
cover all allusion to the ranchman's mishap, but calculated to impress the sheriff with the idea that Bruce
was a highwayman in disguise.

" Yer hand, Mr. Bruce," said Mosely, stepping
quickly forward, with a keen, penetrating glance from
under his shaggy brows, and a grip like a steel claw.
—" Ah, Miss Cynthia ! or is it spring already, and are
the bluebirds with us again ? " he remarked, with easy
gallantry, as his eyes fell upon Cynthia and her muslin dress.

He doffed his broad sombrero suddenly, exposing
his high forehead and scant hair. His hard, blue eyes
were restless and cold, like chilled steel. He twitched
his huge mustaches nervously.

" It'd be a pretty bold bluebird to shake hands like
this with a sparrow-hawk ! " replied Cynthia, with
dimpled audacity, coming quickly forward and holding out a little hand. " Glad to see you, sir ! How
are all the birds down your way—kites, road-runners,
and other jail-birds ? "

" Ho, ho ! " laughed the sheriff, " ye're after me
this time, aren't ye ? Guess ye must hev got up early
this mornin' ? "

" She *did!* " said old Dallas, emphatically, glancing at Bruce—" earlier than I've seen her get up
since the last norther. She was thet anxious about
them bucks this mornin' thet she turned 'em out
afore sun, and run 'em more'n a mile up the creek in
them new slippers I got her for the ' Round-up Ball.'
5

Strange goin's on for a young gal, Mosely—strange
goin's on !"

"Sho !" said the sheriff, laughing. "'Tain't every
day they's a good-lookin' young feller 'round to get up
for.—Is it, Miss Cynthia ? If they were all old and
gray-headed—like me and your old man—I couldn't
blame ye, ef ye never got up !"

He glanced around to note the effect of his words,
but Cynthia had disappeared. At the first allusion
to her early morning ramble, she had stampeded the
fawn and scampered away in pursuit. Mosely turned
and shot a glance at Bruce. He was smoking with
easy nonchalance. But here the approach of the
ebony Amelia, bearing a frothy mixture which looked
uncommonly like a milk-punch, interrupted his reflections.

"Heah am de boss bev'age arter hossback-ridin',
sah !" exclaimed that sable Hebe, handing the tumbler to the sheriff. "Dey ain't nothin' wot goes quite
so fur or strikes quite so neah de spot. It stim'lates
de functions an' 'suscitates de system at de same
time, sah ! Besides," she added, with a crafty wink,
"I didn' wan' to scare yo', nohow, wid de state ob
dat bottle after de egg-nogg dis'pation ob de las'
ebenin' !"

"Let you alone, Amelia, for takin' care of me !"
returned Mosely, draining the mixture with a grateful
smack. "Thet puts a heart in a man d'rectly.—Now,
Al, what's all this about hogs and hosses ?" he inquired, sitting down on an adjacent nail-keg, with a
careless hand upon the butt of a six-shooter, and his
head one side in the attitude of listening.

"Thanks ! Thet's my size, every time !" he remarked, as Bruce rose to his feet, offering him a cigar as he did so.

He bit the end off meditatively.

"Ye needn't go off mad. There isn't anythin' private about this yer bizness—is there, Al?" the sheriff inquired, gazing after the ranchman as he sauntered away.

"Not much ! The more public ye make it, the better I'll like it," returned the elder Dallas. "I want ye to shoot them fellers, or hev this marorderin' stopped."

Bruce did not reply. He was already out of hearing. Ike Mosely glanced critically at his broad shoulders and well-proportioned limbs. In the repose of his youthful strength, he seemed the very incarnation of the sturdy live-oaks among which he strode.

"A likely young feller," said Mr. Mosely, smoking violently and chewing the end of his cigar nervously. "Somehow I rather like his style. In a row I reckon you could count on him. Al, if you're lookin' for a son-in-law thet'd do you and Cynthia both credit, you'll do well to encourage thet chap. He has my best wishes. *He's got sand.*"

And with this official summary of a husband's requisites, he addressed himself to the business before him.

V.

IT was still early morning at the "Mesquite Valley Ranch." A calm tranquillity rested upon the limitless prairie. The scattered files of trees that everywhere straggled across the undulating plain, and gave the locality its distinguishing title, were mute and motionless, as if yet in awe of the recent sunrise. The effulgent sun was lording it over the levels, steeping thicket and chaparral with genial warmth, and projecting the shadows of slowly-moving clouds upon the plain beneath, as in some soft, green mirror. The large pools of water, which at irregular intervals dotted the valley and outlined the course of Indian Creek, were populous with wild-fowl, swinging silently among the reeds and grasses, or rising in noisy company and winging their clanging way across the misty landscape. A few plover piped mournfully from the uplands. The quarrelsome cawing of ravens, holding a stormy conclave in some remote tree-top, at times rose angrily upon the morning air ; and grazing occasionally, at intervals raising his head to regard with attent ears and quivering nostrils the prairie before him, but pursuing a direct course for the distant ranch-house over the sunlit level, a large sorrel horse, saddled and bridled, but riderless, came shrilly neighing.

The house which the horse was thus approaching was large and substantial, and built in the fashion of ranches of the better class. Square in shape, it yet looked from the open prairie a mere box, rising above the vast monotony of the boundless plain. But the curious visitor, who remarked it from a nearer view-point, found it commodious in its appointments, surrounded with a strong barb-wire fence, and flanked by out-buildings and corrals more ambitious in structure than the dwellings of most ranchmen. A broad, sunny veranda ran the entire length of the house, commanding the vast expanse of the outlying valley, as it faded on the right into dim vistas of foliage, tremulous, that morning, with the misty veiling of the coming spring; on the left, into the rugged outlines of the Llano Hills. Over the floor of the porch, where the sunlight lay in broad squares and patches, a half-dozen Mexican saddles were strewed, their bridles slung upon the circular pommels, their broad stirrup-leathers picturesque and embossed. Whips and lariats were lying about. Several colossal rocking-chairs occupied the foreground, with a general air of proprietorship enhanced by their unwieldy bulk. A magnificent buffalo-robe, thrown carelessly over a long reclining chair and warm with the rays of the sun, invited luxurious repose. And above the entrance to the ranch the branching antlers of a deer were fastened, stamping the hospitality of the proprietors with suggestions of the frontier.

The wide doors of the rancho stood invitingly open to the balmy morning air. Within, the broad, bare hallway, with its adjacent doors upon either hand opening into various rooms, was dimly seen. The

walls were picturesque with rifles, revolvers, and ten-
nis-racquets, tastefully arranged and grouped. A guitar, lying carelessly among a heap of cushions on a
comfortable lounge, betrayed by its blue and yellow
ribbons the adornment of feminine fingers. A large
stuffed eagle with extended wings, at the end of the
hall, typified the far-reaching destinies of the Ameri-
can Republic.

A young girl came suddenly to the door and looked
out over the broad valley, shading her brown eyes
against the glare of the sunlight with the fingers of a
jeweled hand. She was tall and stately, and the simple folds of her cloth morning-gown swept to her feet
with a graciousness and ease that betokened position.
The dainty white collar at her throat was fastened by
a single diamond stud that flashed as if in rivalry of
the clear eyes above it. Her brown hair was gathered
in the simplicity of the Grecian knot—the soft tresses,
waving about her temples, were like spun silk. From
the long, dark lashes that swept her beautiful eyes to
the heavily bowed slippers that peeped beneath her
robe, she was all refinement and grace. And the small
handkerchief she raised to her parted lips breathed
that faint atmosphere of odor which seems to identify
the presence of beauty.

She stood quietly a few moments in the corner of
the doorway, gazing out dreamily over the limitless
prospect, at the vast billows of prairie stretching before
her like an emerald sea. Her eyes wore an expression
of wistful tenderness, and there was in them a shade
of disappointment, as one has seen the water of a
liquid pool darker in the shadow of some overhanging
rock. Then she came listlessly forward, and sank

down upon the reclining chair, nestling herself in the soft folds of the warm robe with a little comfortable shudder. Her dark lashes swept her cheek, half hidden in the long fur ; her hands held a vellum copy of verses she had taken from the chair, where it had been thrown carelessly down. But she was not reading ; and the eyes she lifted absently from the book strayed wearily away to the valley. Surely it was very early in the day for reverie and meditation.

The sudden neighing of a horse startled her. She sprang to her feet abruptly, the color mounting to her cheeks and suffusing her neck with blushes, an eloquent delight flashing in her dark eyes. The sorrel horse stood expectantly at the gateway of the rancho, his long lariat trailing from the saddle-bow, his mane and forelock tossed and disheveled with his long wandering.

The girl gazed at him breathlessly a brief moment ; the next, the rosy flush faded from her cheeks, and she stood white as the neighboring wall, her hands clasped before her. She reeled a little, and sat down again in the nearest chair, as if to recover herself.

A few moments she sat thus, trembling violently, her bosom heaving, regarding the motionless horse at the gate with blanched face and agonized eyes. Then there was the sound of footsteps, and a tall, handsome man, with bronzed face and flashing eyes, came striding along the hall and out upon the sunlit porch.

"Why, what's the matter, Edith ? You are not ill, I hope," he said, coming rapidly toward the young lady with an anxious face, as he observed the apparent weakness of her attitude.

"Oh, nothing, Phil!—a sudden faintness, that's all," the young girl answered, striving to rise, a faint color like the flush of dawn struggling to her cheek. She put her hand to her head with a deft, womanly gesture.

"It's so very warm here this morning I can scarcely breathe, and I sat down to rest a moment."

She laughed an anxious, nervous little laugh.

The man regarded her with grave solicitude.

"You don't seem as well lately," he said. "I fear you find this wild life of ours less beneficial than we anticipated ; or perhaps, Edith, you neglect your exercise. We must go to-day for another long prairie canter. Let me call my wife to your assistance."

He turned back to the door of the rancho, and called "Kate!" twice in a loud, imperative voice. There was a musical reply, the sound of a closing door, the hurrying of slippered feet across the bare hallway, and then, with the sudden revelation of a pale-blue morning-wrapper, fluttering skirts, and fly-ing golden braids, the advent of "Kate."

"Just see the state that Edith is in !" said Phil Kernochan, pityingly, directing the gaze of this blonde and radiant apparition to the figure in the chair. "What had we better do with her ? "

He turned as he spoke.

"Hello !" he shouted, his eyes falling for the first time on the sorrel pony standing by the rancho-gate. "There's Hal's pony ! When in the world did he arrive ?" He glanced again at the reclining girl. A light seemed breaking in upon him.

"Why, it can't be," he said in amazement, "that his horse has walked off and left him, and he's been

obliged to lay out a night or two on the bald prairie!
Well, that's rich, I declare!"

He ran hurriedly down the steps of the veranda,
and strode away to the ranch-gate. He threw it
wide open, and the pony, with a whinny of welcome,
trotted gladly within.

Kernochan regarded him critically, taking his
meerschaum pipe from his lips, an amused smile ac-
centing the curves of his mouth beneath his light
mustache. There was no sign of violence or accident. A few cockle-burs clung to the mustang's
mane, an acquisition of his recent travels. The
rolled blanket still hung from the crupper of the
saddle.

Kernochan gathered up the lariat and slung it on
the pommel.

"Rube!" he shouted, turning his head in the direction of the neighboring corrals, where a thick-set
and sun-tanned individual was busy doctoring some
ailing sheep, "give this horse a feed of corn and
groom him a little; take his saddle off and turn him
loose in the door-yard till to-morrow. Don't hopple
him!" he directed, as the man approached in answer
to the summons.

He turned back to the veranda, laughing quietly
to himself, as if some pleasant revelation had dawned
upon him. The fragrant wreaths of smoke from his
pipe rose above his head and brooded in the still,
calm air.

"Well, ladies," he said, coming tranquilly up the
steps, his recent amusement still lingering in his eyes,
"it seems, our careless friend, Bruce, has seen fit to
let his horse come home without him. I suppose

the only thing we can do is to ride out and look him up."

"There, Edith Stafford, I told you that was all it amounted to!" exclaimed Kate Kernochan, smiling reassuringly at the young lady over whom she had been sympathetically engaged ever since his departure. "Give me back my cameo *vinaigrette* this instant! The idea of your being so foolish, dear!"

Miss Edith Stafford languidly extended the article in question — an exquisite blue trifle, carved to represent a crested grebe, and a relic of Phil Kernochan's generosity during his extravagant courtship.

"Do you think, then, he isn't dead?" she inquired, sitting up with sudden animation. "I was certain of it! Oh, dear! I shall never get used to the dreadful uncertainties of this primitive country. I was quite positive some awful crime had been perpetrated." Then, springing eagerly to her feet, "Let us ride out for him at once. Poor fellow, he may be starving to death! I'll put on my riding-habit right off."

She dashed away to the door with a haste that contrasted with her recent feebleness.

"One moment," said Kernochan, catching up a leather quirt from the veranda and flecking his boot with it; "I thought we'd make a hunting trip of this search, and kill two birds with one stone. Ha! ha! starving to death—that's good! You catch Henry Bruce starving to death with a breech-loading shot-gun and matches enough to stock a ranch. Not much! Well, what do you say? There are lots of wild turkey between here and the Colorado

River ; we might take the dogs along and course any that came in our way."

"Oh, that would be charming !" cried Miss Stafford, turning back to flash her gratification upon Kernochan, with a revelation of radiant teeth and eloquent smiles. "Come, Kate, let's hurry and get ready ! We won't be a moment !"

And, with this feminine estimate of that indefinite period allotted to matters of the toilet, the ladies rushed from the veranda.

An hour later they were galloping over the sunlit levels, their cheeks glowing, their pulses thrilling with the exhilarating exercise. Both accustomed to the saddle, they rode with a graceful freedom and dash. Their bay ponies, accustomed to be driven together in harness, seemed to derive a certain pleasure in riding side by side, as if yoked to a chariot, and the ladies, clasping their gloved hands, at times challenged each other to a burst of speed, when they flew along neck and neck until some intervening bush or tree compelled them to break the chain. Phil Kernochan, mounted upon his iron gray, witnessed this graceful revival of the circus-ring with some admiration, and put his horse to his paces to keep the contestants beneath his eye. The dogs—two large, tawny Scotch greyhounds—ranged far ahead, crossing from side to side.

Suddenly a startled jack-rabbit plunged from his form and limped away to the right, his eyes blinking stupid wonder, his exaggerated ears caricaturing his fright. Kernochan charged him with a shout, rising in his stirrups and sending a bullet from his revolver after him, while at full gallop. In an instant the dogs turned, and, catching a glimpse of the fleeing hare, followed in pursuit. Half for the fun of the thing, Kernochan dropped his spurs into the flanks of his gray and started after, calling to the girls to follow.

The jack-rabbit pursued the customary tactics of that remarkable animal. He ran for a few moments at the speed of a railway-train, and with evolutions of his hind-legs that would have done credit to a hay-tedder. Then he stopped abruptly, and with his unmanageable ears, spread like a vessel wing and wing, leered derisively at the following dogs, exhibiting that insolent confidence in his powers of speed which only a jack-rabbit can successfully affect. The next instant, realizing that no ordinary Texan dog was after him, and that the power to annihilate space was not with him alone, he was off like a bolt from a crossbow, quartering suddenly to the right, and easily distancing the greyhounds ; but at a velocity that can only be indicated by saying that the line of his course was visible to the pursuers as a zigzag streak of jack-rabbit.

Meanwhile the mounted party, unable to check their running ponies in their headlong career, swept over the spot where the hare had doubled by several yards. Kernochan was the first to turn, almost lifting his gray with the bit, as he wheeled him sharply round on his off hind-heel, and for an instant was etched against the pale-blue sky—an equestrian statue, with pawing hoofs, flapping sombrero, and flying bridle-rein. In that brief moment he caught a glimpse of Edith, pushing her panting bay to his utmost, and closely followed by Kate. He could not repress a feeling of admiration for the courageous girl as her lithe body swung lightly with the movement of her horse, and a loosened braid of brown hair tossed upon her shoulder. Her eyes were bright with the excitement of the chase, and the face beneath her glossy black beaver, an inspiration of beauty and color.

His eye caught this flying picture as in the flash of a camera. A moment after, a loud whirring and flapping filled the air. Several large, dusky objects rose between him and the ladies, flying in all directions. He caught a glimpse of others running before him in line, their red necks outstretched, their muscular legs rising and falling alternately. They had surprised a small flock of wild turkeys while feeding.

He called to the dogs, already far in advance chasing the fleeing jack, which doubled so quickly and adroitly that they invariably ran over him. The birds were scattering to every point of the compass. Several were still running ahead of him, not yet having taken wing. He turned in his saddle and shouted a warning back to the ladies, who had checked their horses, disconcerted by the scattering of the flying game.

"Follow the bird I take!" came hoarsely back to them, accompanied by some inarticulate sentence about "getting lost." A minute after, they saw the gray horse charge the foremost of the remaining turkeys—an old gobbler, whose iridescent plumes flashed in the sunlight with bronze and gold.

The old bird rose at once in the air, taking wing at first with a strong and rapid flight. They were on the crest of a prairie billow, the valley below being unusually open, dotted here and there with an occasional clump of live-oak. A dark motte of pecans at the upper end of this valley flanked the horizon, and indicated the presence of water.

Down the slope of the slight divide the horses went at full gallop, Kernochan fifty yards in advance.

"Look out for marmot-burrows!" he shouted back, as they charged down upon the open plain. The dogs were with them now, and swept on ahead, their elastic bodies bending double at every bound, their eyes fastened on the gobbler, sweeping still high over their heads, but beginning to droop. At last he came to the ground, fully a mile from where he first took wing, and ran like a scared cat.

After him, over the grassy level, swept the chase in full cry, the dogs gaining upon the turkey at every spring. The bird ran gamely and at a great pace, but with wings outspread and outstretched neck showing his fatigue. He was very heavy and fat, besides being oppressed by the weight of his winter plumage.

Seeing all this, Kernochan urged his horse to his utmost, and was soon close upon the dogs. The turkey rose again, but heavily, passing so near him before he got under way that he struck at him with his heavy quirt in the hope to bring him down. Once in the air, the gobbler wheeled to the right, sailing away this time in the direction of the pecan-grove, as if he hoped to find shelter among the lofty trees. Quickly availing themselves of this change of direction, Edith and Kate turned their horses. In a few moments the three were riding furiously after the flying bird, almost neck and neck.

The bird showed signs of weariness. His legs began to droop. He flew for several hundred yards, dropping lower and lower, his head moving uneasily from side to side.

"After him!" shouted Kernochan, in his excitement rising in his stirrups and urging on the hounds. The hinder dog appeared to gather himself for a second, when he went to the front with a sudden rush, springing clear of the ground and snapping his teeth like a steel trap under the feet of the bird. The turkey drew his legs up convulsively with a sudden cry that showed his alarm.

"Bravo!" cried Edith, lashing her pony at the hound's exploit.

The bird came down shortly after this, and ran desperately, as if for the last time. They were close upon the pecan-grove. All at once the gobbler began to circle. Urging his horse at full speed, his eyes intent upon the coursing dogs and fleeing quarry, Kernochan was suddenly surprised to see the turkey double and rise in the air, coming right back upon them, flying about the height of his saddle, and passing between Kate and himself.

He reined his horse up with all the strength of his body, throwing him flat upon his haunches by the suddenness of the movement. The hounds, surprised by this unexpected stratagem of their prey, ran completely over one another in their efforts to check their onward course. At the same moment, with a rush of wind and a jingle of bit and spur, a horseman passed him flying like the wind. He caught a glimpse of a roan horse, conspicuous for the prominence of his Roman nose and hanging under lip; a strong, well-knit figure, picturesque in flapping sombrero and heavy leathern leggings that reached to the hip; and realized that, as the man passed him, he was gathering up the lariat that trailed from his saddle-bow, as if about to throw it.

In an instant Kernochan had wheeled his gray and was galloping back after the bird. He had scarcely done so, when he saw the horseman swinging his riata about his head preparatory to making a cast. The turkey was just ahead of him, running from side to side, apparently in great distress, its wings outspread, its feathers ruffled, its bill open as it gasped for breath. The man rose in the stirrup and flung his lasso. The long folds of the rope shot forward in a gigantic spiral, falling to earth full on the sloping back of the bird. Hardly had the flying coil left the horseman's hand when the intelligent cow-pony stopped short, bracing his fore feet for the expected shock; but the adroit bird ducked suddenly under the noose, brushing it off with a flap of his great wings. The gobbler swerved suddenly to one side. It was his last effort for life. The hounds, quartering at the moment, met him with open mouth, and catching him fair, dragged the noble bird down amid a cloud of dust and flying feathers.

Kernochan checked his horse instantly, and springing from the saddle, beat the dogs off with his riding-quirt. He raised the great turkey by the legs, but even then was obliged to dispatch it, as it was not yet dead. Fully twenty pounds in weight, the magnificent bird glowed, in the glancing metallic hues of his plumage—a very rainbow of color—a peacock of the plain. He held it aloft with both hands before tying it to his saddle, and turned to share with Kate and Edith in admiring its beauties. As he did so, he was startled by a cry from Kate. She had halted a few yards away, and was seated in the saddle, pointing in the direction of the pecan-motte with her riding-whip, her face pale with anxiety and alarm. A few paces distant the strange horseman was seated quietly upon his pony, engaged in coiling up his lariat and attaching it to his saddle's pommel.

He, too, turned at the exclamation, raising his hand to his eyes to shield them from the glare of the sun. He stared for a moment, gazing out upon the valley ; then, striking his spurs into his roan, with long, loose stirrups and bridle thrown free upon the animal's neck, he seemed to put him in a twinkling at the top of his speed. He vanished from his post with the speed and fury of a meteor. Before Kerno-chan could throw himself into his saddle, he was far out upon the plain.

Lost in astonishment at the mad speed of his de-parture, Kernochan turned inquiringly to his wife.

"Edith!" she gasped, turning upon him a blanched face. "Do you not see her ?"

Following the direction of her outstretched hand, he beheld the cause of the stranger's action. The al-most level valley stretched away in front of him, clear and unbroken, to the dark line of pecans distant about a mile. Across this open a bay horse was running, heading for the timber, and, from the rapid tossing of the animal's head, apparently unmanageable. Its rider, although sitting firmly, had evidently aban-doned the reins, as if the bit were useless or broken, and was endeavoring to maintain her position by grasping the pommel of her saddle with both hands. Kernochan saw at a glance that the horse, whether

6

from fright or excitement, was running away, and
that the situation of the rider was perilous in the ex-
treme.   A misstep, or stumble, or a dash among the
timber for which they were headed, might hurl her
from the saddle and to instant death.   He now understood the headlong haste with which the horseman
had dashed away.

Helpless to stay or avert the terrible danger which
threatened their guest, husband and wife remained
rooted to the spot.   The bay pony still ran recklessly,
with ears viciously laid back, and tail streaming.
Edith, her brown hair shaken loose and tossing upon
her shoulders, the flying folds of her dark habit puffing around her, still clung to her saddle and kept her
seat.   The galloping horseman, closing in upon her
in a long circle, was riding like a centaur, his roan a
thunder-bolt of action against the dull horizon.   A
moment more and he had wheeled in her wake, rising
in his stirrups and lashing his horse a dozen times
with his cruel whip as he rode.   They saw him take
the reins in his teeth, cast off his coat and hat, and,
after a few more blows of his quirt, fling that away
also.   The roan horse, goaded to fury by the blows,
flew like the wind, closing the gap between them at
every spring.   The horseman shifted his reins to his
left hand, standing erect in his stirrups, and urging
him to a final burst of speed.   Kate and Philip caught
their breath.   With a rush the horses seemed to glide
together, the roan passing to the left.   For a second
they appeared as if yoked, straining neck and neck,
and almost flank against flank ; the next, the horseman bent forward, throwing his sinewy right arm
about the girl's waist as she sat in the saddle.   With

a sudden effort he lifted her clear of the saddle-horn, and, as a blow of his boot swerved the bay pony to the right, he bore her away in his embrace, checking his horse as he ran. A second later, halting in the shade of the great pecan-grove, he dropped his fair burden lightly to the ground.

VI

THE vertical rays of noontide were beating down upon Cynthia's bower. Here and there an occasional shaft of sunlight pierced the groined roof, glanced with a golden gleam across the twilight depths, and shivered itself upon the needle-strewn floor in a shower of shining sparks. The leafy ceiling above was bright with a thousand luminous points from the steady glare without. Now and then a cone fell, or a feathery seed-vessel slipped softly to the earth in the gloom of the columned aisles. The sudden bright flash of invading wings, the hurried scampering of a rabbit, or the rustle of some lizard, wakened from his *siesta* on a sun-steeped bowlder, testified the popularity of shade and coolness during the heat of the day. The rattling notes of a banjo, struck at intervals, the low murmur of voices in conversation, and, above all, the odor of burning tobacco, overmastering the aromatic incense of the wilds, announced the presence of other visitors. They were Bruce and Cynthia.

The young girl was seated at the base of a scarred and denuded hemlock, the light sifting through the branches above and falling full upon her head and shoulders. A small banjo, showing signs of abuse and exposure to the elements, lay in her lap. Occasionally she struck the strings. Half reclining at her

feet, and completely enveloped in the wreaths of
smoke that brooded like a blue vapor in the quiet air,
Bruce lay smoking. The antelope-fawn, its feet
curled up, its velvet eyes blinking drowsily; "Aulus,"
his great right paw in a muslin sling, and regarding
his unfortunate predicament with a general flavor of
solicitude and "mustang liniment," completed this
rural quartette.

A sudden breath of air dispersed the smoke, favoring the hound with a passing whiff. He sneezed violently, and looked annoyed, as if the last test had been
put upon his patience.

"You smoke too much, Mr. Bruce," said Cynthia,
waving the passing cloud from the dog's head with a
compassionate hand. "If you keep it up, I wouldn't
wonder ef, one day, you got jest as homely and coffee-
colored as thet skull. Why don't ye quit before it
gets you?"

Bruce laughed, and removed the long amber mouth-
piece of his pipe from his lips. It was of meerschaum, and carved to represent a hand holding a
human skull.

"I don't know," he said, blowing a huge ring,
that shot forward with curling folds until it broke
upon the nose of the nodding antelope. "I suppose
I like to smoke, and then I seem to stand it very well.
Possibly, too, there is something in my associations
with the pipe."

"Who gave it to you, Mr. Bruce?" said Cynthia,
quickly, raising her eyes to his. They were solemn
and deep, and beneath their dark lashes reminded
Bruce of some calm, blue pool he had seen in the
shadow of a wood.

"A friend of mine," he answered, indefinitely, noting her earnestness.

"Yes," she said, "but I meant, was it a man, or wasn't it?"

Her eyes dropped suddenly from his face, and she struck the protesting banjo roughly in her embarrassment.

"It was a lady," Bruce replied, gravely.

"Light or dark complected?" asked Cynthia, breathlessly, not raising her eyes.

"Dark," said Bruce in the same tone—"a rich creamy brown—I don't think that even that beautiful tint there,"—he continued, indicating where the soft white of the stem was faintly dyed—"could hope to vie with her. Her eyes were dark too—more like that," touching the hue of the bowl; "and her hair —there is nothing here to show you that can do it justice."

Cynthia sighed.

"Lawful sakes!" she exclaimed. "An' is thet the reason you're smokin' thet thing all the while, 'cause ye jest naturally expect, one day, to make it look like thet chocolate-colored woman?"

Bruce hurriedly disclaimed any such intention.

"Well, I wouldn't try," she rejoined, "for, by the time you've done it, ye'll prob'ly be dead. Father hed a meerschaum that he was colorin' once, but he said, before he got through, it colored *him* instead. I reckon *so*." After this alarming instance of the effect of nicotine, she became silent. Bruce continued smoking.

"How old is she?" Cynthia inquired, suddenly, turning from him and glancing across the river.

"That's an uncertain question," the gentleman replied. "In fact, I know nothing so difficult to ascertain precisely as the age of a young woman."

Cynthia looked puzzled. Then she apparently received an inspiration.

"Didn't ye get to see her teeth?" she inquired, demurely, but revealing an irresistible circle of pearl by the question.

The gentleman overlooked in silence this query, prompted no doubt by her knowledge of sheep.

"Where does she live?" inquired Miss Dallas, nothing daunted.

"About twenty miles from here," Bruce replied.

"Oh!" said Cynthia. She was suddenly silent. The soft sunlight played amid the tresses of her golden hair, as with downcast lashes she caressed the antelope, burying her fingers in his rough coat. A few needles, shaken from the pines, drifted down upon her. It was as if the fond fathers of the wood were wafting a benediction upon the one who cheered their solitude. High on some rocking bough a blue jay flung his bright pennant, and filled the air with his harsh calling.

Suddenly Cynthia raised her head.

"Do you expect to see her soon?"

"See—whom?"

"Thet girl you're so gone on?" she inquired, with matter-of-fact gravity.

Bruce was about to enter an emphatic protest. In his earnestness he leaned toward Cynthia and took her hand. The girl trembled a little, and the color dyed her cheek, but she did not withdraw it. She lifted her eyes to his and smiled upon him so sweetly, that whatever of mischief there had been in her question fled before it.   Such a radiant beauty had suddenly come to dwell within her eyes.

The quick snapping of a twig caused Bruce to look up.   He dropped the girl's hand abruptly with an embarrassed air.

Two ladies were standing in a sunlit opening without and gazing into the bower.   They were in riding-habits, their long skirts gathered in their left hands, their whips in their right.   The younger of the two—a dashing brunette—was modishly attired. A glossy black beaver, perched saucily on her head, accented the flash of the dark eyes beneath.   The bit of black lace at her throat was fastened with a diamond.   Her hands were fastidiously gloved.   She laughed a merry, ringing laugh, as she advanced into the bower.

"So, sir!" she said, laying her slim gloved hand upon Bruce's shoulder with a certain familiar air of proprietership, "we have found you out at last! And, as usual, surprised you in the attitude of a gallant.   Do not let us interrupt you, I beg; but, at least, favor us with an introduction."

She glanced coldly down at Cynthia, who, intuitively recognizing a rival, returned the glance with the customary feminine cordiality.

"Why, Edith—you here?" exclaimed Bruce, springing to his feet, and clasping the gloved hand in both his own.   "And Kate?" advancing to meet the lady who had lingered without.   "How is this?"

"It means," said Kate, laughing, "that you are a careless, wicked fellow, and that Edith has been half dead with anxiety, fancying you killed or starved to death."

"No such thing!" replied Edith with spirit, lashing a small cedar with her riding-whip in her embarrassment. "I knew all the while we should find him at some farm-house. But I certainly think, Hal," she added, glancing down at Cynthia, who, with lowered crest, had been caressing her fawn and lavishing tender solicitude upon the wounded "Aulus,", ever since the ladies' arrival,—"I certainly think you are very exclusive in regard to your new dulcinea."

Bruce glanced at her with a look in his hazel eyes that was almost reproach. Their eyes met. Edith's expression was one of defiance, but in spite of herself there stole into her dark orbs such a wistful tenderness—such a caressing fondness for the man before her—that she let their curtained fringes drop before his steadfast gaze, and turned her attention to Miss Dallas. An embarrassing pause ensued.

"Cynthia," she heard the cordial voice of Bruce say a minute later, "this is Miss Stafford—the lady of whom I spoke as having given me the pipe. Let me make you acquainted. Also, with Mrs. Kernochan—my partner's wife.

The ladies exchanged salutations, Mrs. Kernochan bestowing a kindly glance upon Cynthia, as her admiring eyes dwelt upon the piquant face in its picturesque setting of red-gold tresses. Cynthia's greeting was frank, but accompanied by a shy restraint that was unusual with her ; Miss Stafford's, disdainful and reserved. Probably her feminine appreciation of the fact that Diana's namesake was both fascinating and pretty, perceptibly lowered the temperature of her recognition.

A few moments later they were all wending their way back to the ranch, Cynthia preceding them, escorted by the gracefully tripping fawn and the limping "Aulus." Bruce accompanied the ladies.

"This picturesque, gypsy acquaintance of yours is quite enchanting, with her quaint simplicity and original pets," remarked Miss Stafford, glancing at Bruce from under her eyelids as they fared on. "I can readily see how easily you forget your former friends."

. "Nonsense, Edith!" Bruce returned with some impatience, breaking a small twig of dry brush as they passed, and hurling it from him violently as if to give vent to his irritation. "This banter and child's play have gone far enough. The little Lone Star maiden is quite a character—a charming little idyl of her native river. I want you to cultivate her and appreciate her originality. She is like a spicy breath from her native woods; she interests me by her very novelty."

"Your eloquence is quite astounding, considering the apathy of your interest," Miss Stafford returned satirically, glancing away in the direction of the low western hills. How indifferent they looked to human disquietude, basking in the warm wintry sunlight!

"But how came she possessed of that beautiful antelope?" inquired Kate, anxious to divert Edith's jealous annoyance. "I quite envy her such a charming companion."

"Isolated as she is," Bruce replied, gravely, "she is not without her admirers. The mother of this fawn, she tells me, was shot by one Buck Jerrold—a cow-boy admirer of hers, I fancy. He found the little thing bleating about the body of the dead antelope, and brought it in to her after one of his hunting trips. Patient nursing and a pious fraud, perpetrated by Cynthia upon an old ewe which had lost her lamb, have enabled her to rear it. I think it a triumphant proof of her cleverness. You see, she tied the skin of the dead lamb around the fawn and quite deceived old ' Granny ' by the trick. Jerrold tells me—"

But here, noticing the surprised look in Mrs. Kernochan's face, he stopped in astonishment.

"Buck Jerrold!" interrupted that lady, turning to Edith ; " why, that explains your gallant friend's knowledge of Hal's whereabouts. I thought his reticence rather singular at the time."

It was now Bruce's turn to appear puzzled.

" You speak in riddles," he said, gravely, regarding them both.

The fair Kate laughed merrily at his bewilderment.

" There have been strange adventures and exciting escapades since you left us, sir," she rejoined, gayly. " You must look to your laurels, Hal, or a sense of gratitude may induce Edith to think seriously of another in your absence. And this Mr. Jerrold is the accommodating equestrian beyond peradventure."

She briefly recounted the adventure of the morning, and the skillful manner in which Miss Stafford had been rescued from her peril.

" Well," said Bruce, with an altered face and an anxious manner, after he had listened to Mrs. Kernochan's thrilling account, given with a woman's enthusiasm and appreciation of detail, "this Jerrold is more of a man than I took him to be, after all. He seemed an odd sort of genius, with certain crotchets unusual upon the frontier, and admirable enough in their way, but I certainly did not look for a hero. However, my dear," he added, anxiously, turning to the petulant beauty who was tripping along beside him, apparently indifferent to the recent conversation in her fastidious avoidance of the thorny brush which threatened her gathered habit, "it seems you found him one."

"Many a loyal heart lurks beneath a ducking-jacket," rejoined that lady, with dignity. "The unlettered men I find among the most endurable of the inhabitants of this primitive country," she added, quickly.

They had reached the ranch-gate and passed within the inclosure. Alcides Dallas, smoking one of Phil Kernochan's long cigars at a precarious angle, owing to the scarcity of his teeth, was seated on a nail-keg under a live-oak, regaling the latter with one of his most dismal fantasies upon the violin.

Mr. Kernochan, discreetly removed to the vantage of the distant door-stone, was preserving the attitude of polite attention, but with a contortion of feature that was distressing to witness. The tableau was so ludicrous and expressive that the party burst into laughter as they joined him. Alcides, seeing that his efforts were producing an erroneous impression, ceased playing at once, and, setting his instrument down, regarded them vacantly, a hand placed idly upon either knee.

"Ye don't seem to ketch on to what I was gettin'

at," he said, vaguely, regarding them with his lack-
luster eyes. " I reckon ye would hev, though, ef ye'd
waited till I got to the ' wind-up.' But ef ye'd known
Marier, ez I did, and hed to live with her, ez I hed,
inter the bargain, I allow there'd been no question."

He paused as if for confirmation. That being not
forthcoming, but his visitors preserving a grave silence,
an apology, it seemed, for their previous rudeness, he
essayed to present his reflections in a more forcible
way.

"It was nigh onto ten years," he said, deliberately, crossing his legs luxuriously as he sat upon the
nail-keg, removing his cigar carefully from its socket
between his sparse teeth, and blowing a volume of
smoke forcibly upon the weed—"it was nigh onto ten
years thet I lived with Marier, and a more hair-raisin'
existence, I'll allow, was never lived by any critter
within the circle of God's providence—"

"Father," said Cynthia, coming forward with a
look of annoyance in her blue eyes, "aren't it almost
time to have dinner? Don't you think you better
put off what you're goin' to say about mamma until
we've all had somethin' to eat, and 'll be better able
to stand it?"

An amused smile went round the circle.

"I reckon so, Cynthy," said her father, rising to
his feet, not without visible regret at her interruption
of his narrative. "What's gone with Ameelyer, natchally? Tell her to hurry up her cakes, and not keep
everybody waitin'. S'posin' we fetch the table out an'
eat dinner in the open air, where we'll hev plenty of
room, bein' ez we happen to be so durned crowded?"
And with this hospitable climax he rolled an inquiring

eye around the assembled company, resting finally
upon Bruce.

"Oh, that would be charming!" exclaimed the
impulsive Mrs. Kernochan, with a little gesture of
ecstasy. "So like a picnic! And to think of our
being able to do it with perfect comfort in the month
of February!—There is something astonishing, Edith,
to write about to your Northern friends."

Forthwith the edict of Alcides was carried to the
ebony Amelia by the delighted Cynthia.

"'Pears like de domestic contrapshuns ob dis yere
ranch am all absquatulated," grumbled that important
personage, as she busied herself in carrying out the
crockery and arranging the table. "De boss am jes'
ez crazy ez de rest ob 'em," she added, darkly, as she
noted old Dallas still violently attacking his cigar, and
watching her preparations with evident satisfaction.
"De fac' is, fo' God, I spec' de ole man's brain hab
been soft'nin' fo' de las' yeah. Ef he keeps up like
he hab been goin' on lately, de reckonin'-day am not
far away."

And, with a gesture of utter bewilderment and disgust, she disappeared in the kitchen.

How signal a success was that picturesque banquet
under the good live-oaks was long remembered gratefully, alike by guests and host. How triumphant
were the achievements of the aged Amelia's cookery,
and how pre-eminently she established her former
claim to actual necromancy in matters of the *cuisine*,
were ever thereafter a matter of frontier history.
The details of that memorable repast are not strictly
a part of this veracious chronicle. We are not called
upon to record how the aged Dallas carved and

lacerated the sinewy body of the noble gobbler that had well-nigh taken his fair pursuer with him to the happy hunting-grounds; how Cynthia arrayed herself in her most gossamer robes, with a view to paralyzing the faultless Edith, and presided at the upper end of the festive board, flanked on either side by the patient "Aulus" and the mischievous fawn; how the great turkey was served in a tremendous dish-pan—it happening that there was no other utensil at the ranch sufficiently large to afford him accommodation; how jokes were bandied as the cheer went round; and how the last drops of the extra-proof whisky which Sheriff Moseley had donated were lavishly poured to crown the cups of cheering egg nog that passed from guest to guest; and how, above the heads of the merry revelers, the hardy Texan oaks bent ever with a sturdy sympathy, and showered their bounty on that rural feast, dispensing a perennial benison of sprays and withered leaves that lent the affair, in the words of Mrs. Phil Kernochan, "a true picnic flavor"—all these are phases of the festivities less to be dwelt upon than imagined.

I must not omit to mention, however, a musical feature of this frontier dinner. It was at that convivial period usually indicated as "across the walnuts and the wine." The afternoon was declining. The short, bright wintry day was losing itself in pensive shadows and gray monotone. Something of the sadness of the approach of night began to fall upon the company, when Mrs. Kernochan proposed singing, probably from a sense of this. After various ineffectual efforts to arouse the table to the attempting of a chorus, she abandoned these in a personal appeal to Miss Stafford and Henry Bruce.

"Come, Edith," said she, "you and Hal must really do something for us ; sing that lovely thing you have been learning lately that is so like a hope of heaven in a field of graves."

Thus bidden, after the usual protestations of being in bad voice etc.— afflictions which I observe affect the amateur vocalist quite as unremittingly as the most capricious *prima donna*—Miss Edith lifted on high a contralto so singularly rich and thrilling, that the very mocking-birds among the live-oaks were stricken mute with admiration. Doubtless they were charmed, too, with the tenor of Henry Bruce, who sang with that appreciative sympathy which often eclipses the work of more accomplished vocalists. About his performance, also, there was a subtle suggestion of being quite in harmony with the beautiful brunette whose voice thrilled so passionately with his. This was very convincing to one of the audience. She sat apart, quite dejected and alone. Her sweet eyes were downcast, and, as she raised them at the close, there was a strange dew upon them, "like woodland violets newly wet." Yet lest you, my dear sir or madam, fail to appreciate the pathos of this affecting duet, I subjoin the words. Read them, since they are eloquent with a faith more cheering than creed or sermon :

"Some day, we say, and turn our eyes
  Toward the fair hills of paradise ;

Some day, some time, a sweet, new rest
  Shall blossom, flower-like, in each breast ;

Some time, some day, our eyes shall see
The faces kept in memory;

Some day, their hands shall clasp our hands.
Just over in the morning lands.

Some day, our ears shall hear the song
Of triumph over sin and wrong;

Some day, some time, but oh! not yet,
But we will wait and not forget—

That, some day, all these things shall be,
And rest be given to you and me.

So wait, my heart, though years move slow,
The happy time will come, we know."

I am afraid, however, that what most appealed to
our little Cynthia, and caused the singular dew above
alluded to, was a certain energy of conviction about
the singing of the musical couple, and an apparent
belief in an earthly "rest," and a "happy time," that
would attend both, albeit their impatient hearts found
the years "moving slow." I am not positive, of
course, but it would seem that the circumstantial evidence pointed to that conclusion. I can only say
that, when the sweet ballad ceased and the little concert was at an end, she was oppressed by a sudden
sense of loneliness and left the banquet quite abruptly.
She hurried away to her bower, there to confide her
disquietude to the circumambient pines. What view
was taken of her agitation by these ascetic mourners
of the wood I can not say. I only know that, after
Cynthia had relieved her overburdened feelings in a
shower of passionate tears, they were as ignorant of
the cause of this sudden melancholy as their *protégée.*

7

Why was she weeping, pray ? She was not in love with this fascinating Mr. Bruce—she, Cynthia Dallas, who knew nothing in nature altogether admirable, save her antelope-fawn, no loyal heart, except the dignified and magnanimous "Aulus." Wherefore, this gratuitous thunder-storm ?

Nevertheless, it was with a feminine conviction that the faultless Miss Edith Stafford had taken her at a very unfair disadvantage, and wounded her in a very sensitive spot by singing so bewitchingly with Henry Bruce, that this Lone Star logician dried her eyes. Had she sung badly, or been guilty of the slightest discord, she could have overlooked it. But, under the circumstances, it was altogether unpardonable. She had been tricked and cajoled ! To be sure she entirely overlooked in her sophistry, the fact that Miss Stafford had known Henry Bruce long before she had been favored with his acquaintance, but she would have dismissed this reflection as irrelevant had it occurred to her. And I think that, through it all, a vivid recollection of the air of ownership with which that lady had laid her gloved hand upon the gentleman's shoulder, when she had surprised them together a few hours since, still rankled in her memory. What right, pray, had she to treat him as if he were some fine-wooled sheep, marked with her "road-brand," and to be claimed as an estray ?

She had lashed herself into a tempest of indignation over this last thought, when she was startled by some one quickly entering the bower. It was Henry Bruce. Cynthia looked up at his strong, athletic figure, and his kindly eyes, beaming down upon her with a certain caressing glance quite inseparable from

his look when interested—a characteristic, by-the-way,
that was very misleading, and had brought misery
to many a confiding feminine heart—and it seemed
to her he had never appeared so handsome before.
Possibly jealousy had made her put on her spectacles.

"Why are you moping here, all alone by yourself,
Cynthia?" he demanded, as if he were reproving
some wayward child. "Don't you know we are
almost ready to go? The ladies are looking for you
everywhere."

"I don't care," the girl replied, with charming
indifference, turning away and hiding her face in the
rough coat of the antelope, which had gone calmly to
sleep during his mistress's recent emotion.

"Why, what is the meaning of this?" inquired
the young man, throwing himself on the ground beside her and taking one of her hands gently in his.
It was snatched rudely away and buried in the fur of
the antelope, but soon reappeared again, with an inde-
cision of movement and lack of repose, that seemed to
say eloquently, "Detain me, if you please!" Bruce
was swift in his deductions. He took pity on the fluttering waif. This time it rested confidingly in both
his own. But the face buried in the fur of the antelope was very restless, as if endeavoring to bore its
way into the fawn's innermost emotions, and, after
some moments of this distressing conduct, Cynthia's
loosely gathered tresses took compassion on their owner
also. Her hair came down and wept in golden rain
upon her shoulders. Her agitation now suffered an
effectual eclipse.

After an interval of what might have been termed

silent communion, during which Mr. Bruce stroked fondly the little fingers within his own, the gentleman hazarded a remark which his knowledge of the facts hardly justified.

"Are you so sorry I am going away, Cynthia ?" he asked, apparently addressing the tumbled mass of golden hair.

The disheveled locks were suddenly agitated by a tumultuous movement that was barely intelligible. Evidently their owner was nodding an assent.

"Why ?" inquired Bruce, ceasing to caress the hand.

A long pause. Finally, the usual reply came apparently from an inaccessible depth, and accompanied by a long-drawn sigh.

"Because."

Bruce smiled to himself—whether from gratification or in irony of the feminine reason, did not transpire. The gentleman, not venturing upon any further inquiry, nor hazarding any additional endearments, the young girl suddenly sat up.

"Do you mean it ?" she said, regarding him wistfully through the mist of her tangled tresses that streamed in her eyes.

"Mean what ?"

"That you are really going ?"

"Certainly."

"What for ?—so as to be with *her* ?"

"So as to get home and attend to my business," Bruce replied, avoiding the issue.

The girl swept her hair out of her eyes with a sudden impatient movement, and leveled her brows full upon him.

"Then *she* hasn't anything to do with it?" she said, with a look of relief.

"She will be in the party, of course, but that is not the reason of my departure," he replied, truthfully enough.

Cynthia was silent, apparently thinking.

"You'll come and see me again?" she said, at length.

"Of course I will—if you wish it."

"I do," she replied, frankly.

Both were silent.

"Henry Bruce," Cynthia said, at last, lifting her eyes to him with a pleading earnestness, "there's going to be a ball over at San Marcus one of these days, and I want you to take me—will you do it?"

"I guess so," the young man replied, indifferently—"that is, if nothing happen to prevent. Have you no other escort?"

Cynthia scowled.

"I never saw the time yet I had to go round begging," she replied, tartly. "Captain Foraker, I reckon, is glad enough to get the chance. *He's* very obliging."

Bruce overlooked the inference.

"When is this remarkable affair to come off?" he inquired.

"About the close of the spring 'round-ups'—some months off yet," she replied, looking at him fixedly, and twisting the antelope's coat in a way that must have been simple torture.

"Cynthia," said Bruce, leaning toward her and looking into her eyes, "I want you to promise me that you won't let that man take you anywhere. You must know, from what your father says, that his company is not creditable to any young woman—much less, yourself."

The girl looked down at the fawn.

"Say *you'll* take me, and I will," she stipulated.

"I have already—conditionally," Bruce rejoined.

"I know that," said Cynthia, "but I don't want any hangin' fire. Are you thinkin' of takin' that dark girl ?" she suddenly inquired.

"Not at all," Bruce answered ; "but business might prevent. I may have to be at 'The Post,' selling my wool ; I might be sick—a thousand things might happen. I can not promise."

"Very well," said Cynthia, rising with decision, but with a disappointed look. "Neither can I. I reckon I hear your sweetheart a-callin' you. P'raps you better be goin'."

And, calling to "Aulus" and the antelope, she whisked suddenly out of the bower.

Bruce returned to the ranch with a feeling of discomfiture. He had the welfare of Miss Dallas sincerely at heart. He had decided to warn her against the attentions of Captain Foraker, of whose indiscriminate and heartless gallantries he had long been aware. But he had met with rebuff, and was naturally chagrined.

He found his companions mounted and impatiently awaiting him. Phil Kernochan was holding the bridle-rein of a small sorrel pony, already saddled for the journey.

Bruce delayed only to shake the horny hand of his host and wave a farewell to the ebony Amelia, who was standing in the doorway of her quarters. Cynthia was nowhere to be seen. Springing into the stirrups of the sorrel, he rode away with the rest, absorbed in his gloomy reflections.

But a hundred yards from the house, what seemed to him to be the loud chirrup of a ground-squirrel caused him to look up, as he rode far in the rear of the cavalcade.

They were just passing a pile of rocks on the crest of a western divide. On the topmost pinnacle of this natural elevation he caught a glimpse of Cynthia, seated in her gossamer robes, an arm thrown about each of her inseparable companions. A light breeze stirred the disheveled masses of her golden hair, which she had not yet taken the trouble to rearrange. She smiled down upon him serenely from the inaccessible height. Bruce waved her a parting greeting with his heavy riding quirt. As he did so, he saw her bend forward eagerly, and, with the rosy tips of her little fingers, fling him a dainty kiss.

VII

SPRING had crossed the Lone Star border. Already the gentle slopes, that bordered the Mesquite Valley Ranch, were donning an emerald livery, and hiding in their sunny hollows an odorous labyrinth of poly-tinted flowers. The live oaks were throwing down upon the brown earth a cloud of sprays and seed-vessels, coloring their dusky leaves with lighter green, and with a cheerful gayety stepping into the opening quadrille of summer. The mocking-birds, crazy with joy, wantoned from every tree-top, flickering to and fro in their half-mourning plumes, and courting their modest sweethearts with a deliriousness of melody that was very contagious. Even the jack-rabbit, roused from his form by the stumbling wayfarer, had less of sarcasm than common in his droll blink, as he limped away. Mirth romped in the valleys, and laughed on the divides. And domestic life at the Mesquite Valley Ranch took on a livelier interest as the season demanded.

But the plans of that good fellow, Phil Kernochan, had met with disappointment, and he chafed with chagrin, and pulled his blonde mustache in his most approved, nervous manner, as was his habit when business vexed him. He had intended building a large barn and stable that should rival, in the mag-

nificence of its appointments, the commodious ranch
of which he was so justly proud. The cellar had'
been dug, the timber purchased and carted, the car-
penters and assistants hired, when his builder—the
man to whom he had confided all his pet schemes and
projects—suddenly died of apoplexy. Kernochan
was highly indignant. The misfortune put him out
of all patience with the genial and forward season.

He burst abruptly into the sitting-room, one bright
April morning, with an open letter in his hand, quite
startling Edith, who was writing at a small escri-
toire, and even causing Bruce, who was playing the
guitar, to narrowly escape dropping the instrument.

"Well, upon my word, Phil!" the latter remonstrated. "What's the matter?"

"Matter enough!" Kernochan rejoined, surlily.
"Here's my boss-builder, the man I relied on to put
those improvements through, gone and died just when
I was about to begin. It's rather rough papers on the
head of the house!" He threw the letter on the floor,
thrust both hands into his pockets, and strode away
to the window.

Bruce took a long puff at his cigar before he replied, but his hazel eyes twinkled with the humor of
the situation.

"I presume, inasmuch as you had taken the trouble to get everything ready for him, you regard it as
rather disobliging in him to die—not to say unprin-
cipled," he replied, with quiet sarcasm. "I say, Phil,
I have an idea!"

"Keep it!" returned Phil; "you'll need it before we get through with this business."

"I had hoped," said Henry Bruce, with mock

gravity, " that I had emigrated too far south, at last, for any one to attempt to perpetrate that venerable 'chestnut' upon his fellow-man. But I see I am a victim of misplaced confidence. I must have a short canter to escape any disastrous effects.—Edith, what do you say to a little trip this morning on horseback? I lost my meerschaum yesterday, somewhere between here and the lone camp at the 'Soldier's Water-Hole.' I thought I would go out and look it up.

"The pipe I gave you, do you mean?" Edith inquired. "Then, that's the last of it, rest assured. I should be glad enough of the ride, but a more evident wild-goose chase was never attempted. You are not serious, Hal, that you expect to find it?"

"Why not, pray?" Bruce rejoined. "I know the general direction, and, if necessary, can trail my horse's tracks. I have not a doubt I shall find it. It is only a matter of five miles—a mere *bagatelle*. I found five newspapers and a letter I lost once, pony-back, over twice that stretch of country."

"Well, I do not mind accompanying you, to show you how absurd the effort is, if for no other reason," Miss Stafford replied. "There!" pounding the stamp on the envelope she had just directed with her dark, jeweled hand. "Wait for me at the gate, and have the horses brought around. I'll be down in a minute."

It was a bright morning, so clear that the Llano Mountains, on the farther horizon, seemed distant scarcely a stone's-throw. The air was redolent of perfume and warmth. The scissor-tails, baring their rosy bosoms to the sun, sat upright in the tops of the mesquites at every turn, surveying the emerald landscape with a dignity and serenity worthy of a much larger bird. At times they ventured upon a slow and labored flight, piloting their trailing plumes like some spent arrow too heavily feathered. A few summer duck—the harlequin camp-followers of that army of water-fowl that had beset the creeks and pools in the early season—whirred away as they approached each prairie water-course.

Bruce and Edith checked their horses in a grassy valley, opening before them in long vistas of portulaca and wild verbena and purple "buffalo-clover." A delicious odor rose upon and enveloped them. The feet of their horses seemed to be treading perfume. They were literally swimming in a sea of scents far more delicate than the rarest treasures of Rimmel or Lubin.

Edith inhaled the sweet air, and drank in the tropical luxuriance of the prospect with a cry of delight.

"How beautiful!" she exclaimed. "I declare, Hal, it seems a pity to ride through this natural parterre."

"Why so?" returned Bruce, with a man's indifference for the delicate and perishable. "Besides, there are acres and acres, just like this, that we shall never see."

They sat regarding the prismatic hues of the valley, stretching before them in one woven carpet of color. A small, cotton-tail rabbit, that had been eying them from the vantage of a neighboring bush, was taken with a sudden panic and skurried away through the purple billows, leaving the track of his frightened course visible in a tossing wake.

"If you dropped your meerschaum in any such tangle as that, Hal," said Miss Stafford, following the animal by the sudden commotion among the flowers, "we may as well give up the search at once."

"Granted," replied Bruce, courteously, patting his pony's neck ; "but you see, my dear, I didn't. I merely brought you down this way to show you what Texas could do in the line of landscape-gardening. I doubt if you find its equal anywhere in the East."

"You are very considerate as well as endearing, this morning," the young lady replied. "Why is it you invariably choose these remote situations to display your affection ? You might, at least, give me the satisfaction of an audience."

Bruce was silent a few seconds. He did not appreciate Miss Stafford's raillery when he dispensed with the conventionalities.

"It is always your way, Edith," he said, reproachfully, "to meet all sincerity with skepticism and caprice. These complimentary speeches, delivered to order, and in the presence of others, have little to recommend them but flattery ; and you are well aware of it."

"They are none the less agreeable to a woman's vanity," replied the fair equestrienne, turning her horse aside to peer into the nest of a mocking-bird in a dwarf mesquite.

The courageous thrush flew at her with trailing wings, forcing her to strike at it with her riding-whip.

"Ah ! Hal," she said, raising a finger at him archly when this little episode was over, "that is a singular organ, that susceptible heart of yours. Quite a remarkable piece of mechanism in its way. What

with your Northern *inamoratas* and these Texan
heroines, it must be pretty well honeycombed by this
time."

Bruce laughed.

"There are traces of old scars," he said, gravely,
as they rode on together, "but it is still intact, my
lady."

"Can you still be sent on errands as formerly ?"
she inquired, stopping suddenly.

Bruce reined up his mustang.

"On yours—always," he said.

"As gallant as ever, she returned. "I thought for
the moment you were addressing Miss Dallas."

"As *sincere*," said the young man with emphasis,
not noticing the implied satire of her last remark.

"Well, then," said the careless brunette, the color
dyeing her clear, olive complexion as she turned toward him, her beautiful face flushed with the exhilarating exercise, "I dropped my riding-whip, I think,
just after my encounter with that bold little bird a
few rods back. Won't you ride back, please, and
verify your pretensions to wood-craft ?"

She pushed one little foot free from the folds of
her habit as she said this, and critically regarded the
silver spur with which it was adorned. She had a preoccupied, serious air.

Bruce glanced at her admiringly as she preferred
this modest request. The little, glossy, black beaver
had not been put into requisition that morning, there
being no likelihood of feminine criticism, and con-
sequently no necessity for overawing envious womanhood with the faultlessness of her get-up. She wore,
instead, a velvet turban—the product of her own taste

and ingenuity—surmounted by the extended wings
and tail of a blue jay. It was mightily becoming.
Miss Stafford knew it. She was also aware that she
was never more fascinating than when on horseback.

This conviction dawned upon Bruce as he caught
the graceful curves of her lithe figure, the soft glow
of health in her cheek, the languorous light of her
dark eyes, and the brown masses of hair but carelessly
confined and slipping to her shoulder. He put spurs
to his mustang and was soon riding about where they
had halted, trampling down the clustering flowers in
the vain attempt to secure the missing whip.

Miss Stafford remained quiet in the saddle without
looking back. There was a mischievous smile about
her coquettish mouth. Her hands toying with her
pony's mane, she became interested in studying the
movements of a chaparral-cock that sat shading himself beneath the filmy veil of a budding mesquite.
The monkish bird had evidently returned from early
mass, and had not yet recovered from the solemnity
of the ceremony. His very piety seemed to oppress
him. He turned his grave head from side to side,
like a gloomy friar beneath his cowl—"each eye a sermon and his brow a homily." It was evident that
the promise of his youth had been blighted by the
vanity of all earthly things.

The young girl soon wearied of his somber gravity.
Then she drew from some extemporized hiding-place
the missing whip. She held it critically in her gloved
fingers. The ivory handle bore a crest with shield
and chevron, and the legend, "*Fac et Spera.*"

The quick snapping of a twig caused her to look
up. She caught her breath with a sudden murmur of

delight. Scarcely ten yards away a magnificent buck had halted in the act of crossing her path, startled by the apparition of her mounted presence.

The beautiful creature stood knee-deep among the flowers as if suddenly turned to stone. His branching antlers had that soft, tender bloom that is almost painful to the spectator, and technically known as "the velvet." His wide-open eyes stared at the intruder, and the delicate, quivering nostrils alone gave evidence of the graceful bounding life sleeping in the delicate limbs.

For nearly a minute they quietly confronted one another, and a critical observer would have been puzzled to determine in which there was more of beauty—the startled, steadfast gaze of this forest paragon, or the rapt, fascinated expression of the gazelle-eyed girl. Then the tension of the breathless tableau grew annoying. Miss Stafford raised herself in her stirrup, and flung her whip at the breathing statue with the impotence of womanhood.

The deer started, took a neighboring bush with a leap of exquisite grace, and, a second after, was visible only as a dusky object, flying with the speed of the wind down the many-vistaed valley, and waving a white banner that caricatured the fleetness of its movements.

The animal had scarcely taken its arrowy bound, when a rifle cracked, and a bullet came whistling by the startled Edith, clipping a twig a short distance in front of her.

She turned in her saddle. Bruce was riding toward her, restoring a small carbine to its leathern holster as he rode, a faint blue smoke still streaming from the muzzle. There was the spice of gunpowder on the morning air.

"What on earth did you frighten him for ?" he said, petulantly, as he rode forward and dismounted to pick up the fallen whip. "If you had not sent me back on that fool's errand, I should certainly have shot him."

"You mean to say you would have killed the beautiful thing, you cruel fellow ?" almost screamed Edith, taking the restored missile without an apology for her previous duplicity. "I'm glad I did it, then. However, I thought you ought to be reminded, sir, that it was the 1st of April. You are in altogether too high feather this morning to be endurable."

They turned into a narrow trail between two sloping hills. A large pecan motte was visible at its farther end, making the little cañon a veritable *cul-de-sac*. Suddenly a volley of shots from cracking " sixshooters " startled them from the non-committal quiet that had fallen upon them. A few yards in front of them a drove of piebald hogs charged wildly down the hill, followed by several horsemen fiercely shouting, and shooting into them at every leap of their running mustangs. The coarse bristles of several of the fleeing porkers were laced with blood.

Edith clasped her hands in dismay, her pony stopping short in his tracks at this sudden apparition of bloodshed. In a few seconds the noisy chase had swept through the cañon, the mounted men scarcely noting them in the excitement of the pursuit.

Bruce reined up his horse with an angry jerk upon the bridle.

There is Lem Wickson's lawless gang again !" he exclaimed. "And, as usual, at their old tricks."

He dashed away a few paces into the underbrush. A large boar had fallen in the thicket, faint from loss of blood. Weak as it was, the fierce animal raised itself upon its haunches and glared at him with its wicked eyes, gnashing its distorted tusks besmeared with blood and foam. Bruce recognized at once the conspicuous "paint-brand" of Alcides Dallas—a large red "A. D." upon the animal's hip.

He rode back to Edith with a grim look upon his usually frank features.

"This sort of thing will not do, little woman," he remarked, raising his broad hat and wiping his forehead.

"Why don't you write them a note and tell them to stop it—that you do not like it, at all ?" Edith advised, with a knowledge of frontier etiquette that was ingenuous and charming.

"How would you word it ?" inquired her companion, a smile struggling to his lips in spite of his irritation. "Something like this? 'Mr. Henry Bruce presents his compliments to Mr. Lemuel Wickson and his assistants, and regrets to say that he personally objects to their shooting stray hogs on his premises ?' It strikes me that is precisely what the occasion demands—some such delicate treatment. Thanks for the suggestion !"

"Oh, bother !" replied Miss Stafford, blushing bewitchingly under his irony.

"I'm afraid, Edith, you do not appreciate the frankness of popular feeling in respect to outrages of this kind. When this return to barbarism is detected

8

upon the frontier, especially if, as in the present case, horse-stealing is united to the misdemeanor, a lariat and a live-oak limb is the usual form of remonstrance."

"You mean they hang them?" said Edith, breathlessly.

"I mean that Judge Lynch usually decrees that penalty."

"How dreadful!" exclaimed the girl, whipping up her pony smartly and dashing away, as if to escape the recollection.

"One moment, Edith!" shouted Bruce, spurring after. "We—are—about—approaching—our—rendezvous." He enunciated his words with difficulty as their horses plunged forward.

"Pardon me!" said Miss Stafford, seeing this, and stopping at once. "What have you to say?"

"We are near the 'lone camp,'" said Bruce, halting also. "You may possibly get a momentary glimpse of a queer being—one of the strangest instances of ill-starred destiny that I have ever met—a college-bred man, mature, able-bodied, and withal the best-read and most cultured individual it has ever been my fortune to meet."

"You astound me!" said the girl, her eyes wide with amazement. "Such a man as you describe, herding sheep at twenty dollars a month?"

"Exactly. A man who quotes Milton with fluency, and who draws upon his memory when he wishes to consult Shakespeare and Byron."

"Why, tell me about this wonderful shepherd," Edith requested; "he interests me."

"There isn't very much more to tell, except that he is something of a hermit, seems to prefer this sort of solitary life, and reads, all the while, the oddest books you can imagine. I found him poring over Apuleius the other day. He's a sort of 'Manfred,' with his satanic gloom left out. Now I think of it, didn't it strike you as strange that Cynthia should have named that old hound of hers 'Aulus'? I puzzled over it a good deal. I understand, however, that this old fellow gave her that dog when it was only a pup. At any rate, the donor answers to his description. The mystery now is perfectly clear. Don't you remember, in Macaulay, 'Aulus the dictator—the man of seventy fights?'"

"Yes, indeed — what an excellent name! It haunts you. And I suppose the character of that dignified monster is thoroughly in keeping with his cognomen."

"Quite, I imagine. Cynthia tells me that she never goes to San Marcus that he does not attack and whip half the dogs in the village."

They had reached the "lone camp" at last. Its appearance was forlorn enough—a small tent, stained and discolored with the weather, its cords relaxed, its open fly fluttering in the wind ; within, a few tumbled blankets and articles of clothing, presided over by a hurricane-lantern tied to the ridge-pole and permeating the interior with its odor of kerosene. The scant cooking-utensils of the solitary were littered about—an iron pot containing boiled beans, a skillet, several empty tomato-cans, and a dilapidated frying-pan that had seen better days. These refugees of the kitchen were broiling in the noontide sun. A side of bacon hung from a neighboring tree. But no trace of the occupant of this dreary outpost of civili-

zation was visible about the ashes of the camp-fire
that betrayed his former presence.

"Do you mean to tell me," said Edith, with an
expression of disgust, that a man of such tastes as
you describe, passes his days in such a den as this?"

"Yes," replied Bruce—"and without complain-
ing. He seems to desire nothing except what will
satisfy his bodily wants. I am sorry that he is not
about, so that you might have a glimpse of him.
Perhaps we will fall in with him on the way back."

They rode rapidly away. Half-way down the little
cañon they passed an odd figure, sitting remote and
lonely upon a high rock, and smoking a short clay
pipe. He was without a coat, and had thrown about
his shoulders a gray blanket, extemporized for a gar-
ment. He wore a large slouch hat, somewhat battered
and faded by exposure to the weather. His long, unkempt, gray beard streamed down upon his breast,
and his eyes had a wild and frenzied expression. His
scant trousers were worn through in places, exposing
a substratum of red flannel at the knees, and between
the tops of his hobnailed shoes and his retreating
breeches was an appalling display of gaunt and re-
luctant ankles. One might have been pardoned for
imagining that the bare apparition of these monstrosi-
ties had struck terror into his nether garments, im-
pelling them to beat a hasty retreat up the calves of
his legs.

When they were riding down the cañon again,
Bruce asked Miss Stafford what she thought of his
literary peripatetic.

"I hardly know what to say," said she, checking
her pony by the side of a small spring that brawled

over its pebbly bed, and dripped its tinkling overflow into a rocky basin. "The idea of a walking encyclopædia and dictionary of poetical quotation here in the wilds! And to think of that creature burning the midnight oil, as he must, to have acquired this knowledge, and wasting his sweetness on the desert air in this agonizing fashion—it is too dreadful! I verily believe, from what you tell me, that the man is another Macaulay, and that he might hope to realize his famous boast and reproduce the 'Paradise Lost.'"

It was very still. The soft tones of her animated voice had died away. Only the musical clink of the fountain, knocking its silver heels against the rock as it tripped gayly on its way; while, a solitary mocker, perched upon a filmy mesquite-spray, attempted a liquid measure in rivalry at infrequent intervals. The blue sky bent brightly overhead.

Somehow a strange ecstatic feeling woke in the heart of the young man as he sat in the saddle, gazing at the bright face before him framed against the soft, green foliage of the budding trees. There was nothing in her words to awaken it. Surely Milton and Macaulay are not cup-bearers to Cupid. Yet they lingered aimlessly by the laughing fountain. Anon a bright-winged butterfly—it might have been the airy Psyche of the mischievous god himself—came floating through the sheltered coolness of the grove upon its listless pinions:

> "Sweet, sweet, sweet god Pan!
>   Blinding sweet by the river!
> The sun on the hills forgot to die,
> And the lily revived, and the dragon-fly
>   Came back to dream by the river."

Miss Stafford had drawn off the little kid gauntlet she had worn all the morning, and the small brown hand, "all heavy with its weight of rings," rested lightly on the saddle-pommel.

"Edith," said Bruce, leaning forward in his saddle, and taking the soft fingers in his, "I have long wished to tell you something."

The "cool, flower-like hand" rested a second in his own burning clasp. It was as suddenly withdrawn with a little triumphant cry.

"Why, there it is, after all!" she said, pointing to something lying among the moss at their horses' feet. Bruce, thus suddenly recalled to the present and the practical, looked quickly down. The lost meerschaum, with its grinning skull, stared up at him from the ground below. Was ever Love's communion interrupted by discovery so *mal à propos!*

VIII.

A TRIO of mounted men rode up to the "Mesquite Valley Ranch." They were dusty and travel-worn, and the horses they bestrode were jaded and flecked with the foam of hard riding. At the ranch-gate they halted, and the central figure of the group—a small man with a slouching seat in the saddle—removed his distinguishing sombrero, and wiped the perspiration from his high forehead.

"By the Lord!" he exclaimed, dashing a hard, small hand across his eyes with a quick, impatient gesture, "how the sun glares to-day! Whether it's my bein' up so much nights, or thet Lampasas whisky, I kin skursely see my hand afore my face. Dick, chuck me over thet flask of 'tarantala-juice'!"

Thus commanded, the individual addressed—one Mr. Jake Sharp, of choleric memory—extracted from his ducking-jacket a large tin pocket-companion, known on the frontier as a "silent comforter," and tossed it to his comrade. He was a big, muscular man of the Herculean type, and he flung the flask from him as if it had been a feather. The other caught it deftly.

"A-ah!" ejaculated the first speaker, clearing his throat after throwing his head back and partaking

freely of its contents, "that stuff takes hold, whether
it's damagin' or otherwise. I feel refreshed a'ready.
'Humly Jim,' will you irrigate?"

The third party, addressed by this uncomplimentary title, exhibited the customary frontier alacrity in
alcoholic matters, and reached out a hand for the
liquid refreshment, more or less disfigured by scars
and "tetters."

He was not a prepossessing object. His long, lank
hair fell down upon his coat-collar. His beard was
straggling and untrimmed; and his nose was gone,
—that is to say, the nostrils were there, but only in
the shape of two rifts or fissures in his disfigured face,
the bridge of that distinguishing feature having been
literally plowed away by a six-shooter bullet in a duel
at close quarters.

Despite the disorder of his dress, due to dust and
hard riding, the small stature of the first speaker, his
heavy mustache, bald forehead, and nervous manner
revealed Sheriff Mosely of Oskaloo. He blew the few
remaining drops of spirit from his huge mustachios,
and tweaked them fiercely as he dismounted.

"I reckon we better tie up till the sun gets down
a little," he said to his companions. "I ain't very
well known here, but if thet chap, Kernochan, is as
likely a feller as his pardner, Henry Bruce, we won't
get no slouch of a reception. Ye might give 'Smithareens' a feed of corn afore ye come in."

With this considerate suggestion for the welfare
of his mare—a long-limbed, gaunt, ill-favored roan—
he unslung his revolvers from his saddle-pommel, and
strode away to the porch, buckling on his holster-belt
as he went.

The afternoon sunshine was slumbering on the broad veranda. A pair of Scotch greyhounds raised themselves lazily from the door-stone, and barked at the stranger. The quick rustling of a woman's dress, and a vision of fluttering ribbons and flying braids, as she hurried into the house, indicated that the fair Kate had also been surprised by the arrival.

"Dog gone it! thet's a woman all over!" exclaimed the sheriff, halting in his tracks, and patting the heads of the dogs who fawned upon him. No dumb animal could long resist the approaches of Ike, much less anything of the canine type. He possessed the true sportsman's touch, and they detected it at once.

"Thet's a woman every time!" continued Mr. Mosely, confiding a knowing wink to the posts of the front gallery. "She's prob'ly gone in to slick up. It's no use, tho'! I've been tryin' to impress it on the female sex, fur the best part of a wearin' life, thet they hain't no power, natchally, over the Sheriff of Oskaloo."

In spite of the emphatic protest of Mr. Ike Mosely in regard to the invulnerability of his affections, it was quite noticeable that, having mounted the steps, he took the opportunity of surveying his warlike undersize in the soft mirror of the ranch-window, and actually passed his short fingers through his scanty locks, as he sank down in the luxurious reclining-chair. A small handkerchief with polka dots—one of those delicate trifles that femininity affects—was crumpled up in the fur of the great buffalo-robe. Ike took it up carelessly. It was redolent of a delicate perfume, and pleasantly suggested the owner. He raised it reverently to his lips.

"We don't get very much of this biz'ness in our profession," he soliloquized, "but it's humanizin', and makes a man remember who he is."

He became strangely quiet, and his hard, steel-blue eyes took on a softer look, as the faint odor woke a chord of his memory. What was it about the scent of those orange-blossoms that took him back in the past? He saw an old plantation-house, and its out-lying fields of corn and cotton. The moon rose softly over the bayou, tipping the low porch with black and silver. Who was that standing in the shadow there, the vines of the trellis drifting in patches over her fair young face? And who that young fellow, small of stature, but lithe and active, slipping upon the lit-tle hand a circlet of gold beneath the pale moon's glamour? Ah, yes! it was all past long ago! There was a small green mound out by the lagoon, which the "sentinel cypress-tree stands over." And the willows wailed a low dirge by the hurrying stream. It was all gone long ago! But somehow the rough sheriff, for all his brusqueness, found the sunlight too strong for his eyes again, even upon the shady veranda, and shielded them against it with his heavy hat-brim.

A step on the porch recalled him. It was Henry Bruce. He came toward him with an outstretched hand and a frank greeting.

"Well, well, Sheriff Mosely, glad to see you've got over our way at last," he said, cordially, with a hearty hand-shake. "Which way this time?"

"On the way hum, now," Mosely rejoined, return-ing the grip with sinews of steel. "Badly done up, too, and gen'rally knocked out by the experience of the last three weeks. Me and my two depyties hev

been down on the stage-road, layin' fur road-agints day
and night. We had a brush with 'em night afore last,
and done pretty well, but Humly Jim got a bullet
through his hand, and Jake Sharp lost a finger. I
ain't been in a bed fur a dog's age."

"Any one killed?" inquired Bruce, knowing the
sheriff's delicate habit of avoiding the fatal details in
these midnight encounters.

"Lessee?" said Mr. Mosely, putting his head on
one side, closing his eyes, and apparently indulging
in a sincere effort of memory. "I disremember exactly whether it was three or five of them fellers passed
in his chips. I got two, I know, with thet new self-
cockin' Colt's, ole man Dallas give me. Geewhittaker!
but thet are a pretty boy to shoot, natchally; beats
the ole fashion of filin' the tumbler all to death.
Humly Jim called one chap in with his Winchester—
the best line-runnin' shot I ever see; by good luck it
was the one who winged *him*. And Jake— How
many *did* you git, Jake?" he inquired, as the two
deputies lounged slowly up the steps of the porch, and
perched on the low railing.

"None," said Jake, sullenly, "not a mother's son
ez I knows on; my hand was bleedin' so like all possessed thet I hedn't any use fur a six-shooter."

He exhibited the stump of his finger, bandaged in
a bloody rag. It was now apparent that Humly Jim
had also suffered in the night encounter. His left
arm was worn in a sling.

"Ef this yer foolishness continners," remarked
Mr. Mosely in a disgusted tone, surveying his wounded
subordinates, "the gals in this country will hev to put
on their spectacles to find a sound, able-bodied man

into it. They ain't a fightin'-man in Oskaloo thet's got the average allowance of fingers and toes. Some's without ears, and they's a few "—chuckling softly to himself—"ez is losin' their hair, but the majority o' *them* are married."

As the sheriff concluded, he gravely uncovered his scanty locks, and rubbed his bald pate with his red bandana.

"N-n-nobody can a-allow thet a gal relieved you o' y-y-yourn," stammered Humly Jim, with a spasm of merriment as malevolent as the laugh of a hyena.

"Not much!" said the sheriff, shortly. "They was a gal once who was a little soft on me, and she said to me, 'Oh, how I wish I hed your hair!' I hed more of the article then than I have now," Mr. Mosely remarked, apologetically. "She said *thet* from a spirit o' gush, I reckon, but meanin' it, all the same, ye know; howsomever, I didn't cotton. I suspicioned thet gal to hev designs on my futur' state, and reckoned I'd give her a hint thet I was onto it. 'Sal,' sez I, 'ye kant hev my scalp nohow, much as ye admire it.' She never hed much to say to me arter thet."

"To change the subject somewhat, gentlemen, from the fair sex to more vital interests," put in Henry Bruce, "I fear your labors are not yet over. I surprised Lem Wickson and his gang, this morning, engaged in their old pastime of hog-hunting on my range. The hogs, they were shooting, belonged to Alcides Dallas, and had his 'road-brand.' They were over by the 'Soldier's Water-Hole,' on the 'Twin Divides.'"

"Ye don't say!" said Mr. Mosely, rising upon his

elbow excitedly, as he received this intelligence. "Is it possible them fellers are in thet biz'ness yet? They must be hankerin' fur a term in jail at the 'Post,' and Lem, I reckon, is lookin' forward to bein' the principal figure in one o' them 'necktie matinées' thet I've presided at more frequent lately than I hev any use fur. Leastwise thet's wot he'll hev to attend ef he keeps on with this hoss-stealin.'"

"I'm too tuckered out jest now," continued Ike, sinking back in his chair with an air of fatigue, "and my possy is too badly used up to push things right away. I'll hev to enter a '*nolly prosequy*' fur the present. But, howsomever," said he, rising up again excitedly, and laying a significant hand on his revolver, "I'll run thet Lem Wickson down afore I'm a month older, or my name's not Mosely. Thet man is gettin' on the inside track of my moral principles by his impudence, and thet's suthin' I won't allow no one to do. Besides, I owe thet much to 'Allsides' himself."

Sheriff Mosely's righteous outburst of indignation was interrupted by the sound of footsteps and voices as Mrs. Kernochan and Miss Stafford came out upon the veranda. The usual courtesies were exchanged, the bluff sheriff exhibiting an off-hand gallantry in meeting the ladies, which invariably surprised those who knew the man and the rough duties of his calling. Far different was the bearing of the deputies, Jake Sharp and Humly Jim, who were instantly surprised into that uncouthness which overtakes the uncultured male animal in the presence of beauty and refinement. They descended abruptly from their perches, executed the customary awkward salutation,

and then, climbing back upon the railing from sheer
embarrassment, were overcome by a painful silence
and a conviction of being all hands and feet.

"You were speaking of Alcides Dallas, Mr. Mosely," Mrs. Kernochan remarked, sitting down in one
of the large, old-fashioned rockers. "How is that
queer old man and his quaint little daughter? Does
he entertain visitors as much as ever with his bewilder-
ing music upon the violin?"

"Having just returned from a professional visit
down in the lower country, I can't really say just how
they *are* gettin' on over by the Colorado," replied the
sheriff, with a humorous twinkle of his blue eye, that
showed he appreciated the lady's comment, "but I
suppose the usual overtures to 'Courtship' and 'Matri-
mony' are still in order. By-the-way, are you ladies
aware that there is to be a ball given at San Marcus
immediately after the 'spring round-ups'? It can't
be more than a fortnight away, and such another opportunity for a stranger in the Lone Star to witness
the gayeties of the season is not often afforded.—You
must ask Mr. Bruce to escort you," turning to Miss
Stafford.

"A ball!" exclaimed the fair Edith, who had
been leaning against a pillar of the veranda, listening listlessly to the previous conversation, "a
genuine frontier merry-making, such as I have heard
so much about? That is delightful! I must
see it by all means!—You will take me, Hal, of
course?"

"I suppose so," replied Bruce, in rather a hesitating
tone, on being thus directly appealed to. "I hope
you won't think me rude, Edith, but the fact is I

have already part-way committed myself in regard to that affair."

"And to whom, pray?" inquired Edith, raising her pretty brows in the completeness of her surprise. "What siren has anticipated me in this request, I should like to know?"

"Oh, it's a little favor Miss Dallas requested during my visit there," Bruce responded, carelessly enough. "I'm sorry these engagements conflict, however. What do you think I'd better do about it?"

"Do about it?" returned Miss Stafford, with a proud toss of her head. "Why, you'll take *me*, of course. You'll write Miss Dallas a note—I'll write it for you if it's too much bother—in which you'll say that your first duty is with your guest, and that she won't release you under any circumstances. *I won't!* I think that disposes of the matter very satisfactorily," she concluded, with a certain triumphant smile of superiority, which would have charmed the absent Cynthia, had she been privileged to witness it.

"I'm afraid Cynthia will regard that as coming with a very ill grace from me," Bruce rejoined, as if thinking aloud. "However, there is considerable force in what you say.—By-the-way, sheriff," he said, suddenly, as Mr. Mosely rose with a quick glance at the sun, as if about to take his departure, "do you happen to be going in the direction of the 'Dallas Ranch'?"

"Well, I do happen to be ridin' that way," Mosely replied.—"I was about to say, ladies, that I regret professional duties will prevent my offering my personal services in the present emergency." The sheriff belonged to that recognized class of individuals whose vocabulary improves with their surroundings. " But that being, unfortunately, out of the question, Mr. Bruce, if I can take any message to Miss Cynthia, or do you any other favor, I'm here to do it ! "

" No message is necessary—thanks ! " Bruce rejoined in rather an emphatic tone ; "and I feel a natural reluctance about making the request I do. The fact is, I think a guitar would be such an improvement upon that poor, weather-beaten banjo, Miss Dallas possesses, that I should like to send her my own. I think, with her knowledge of the banjo, she will readily learn to play upon it. But it's an awkward thing to carry in the saddle, sheriff."

" Bless your soul, man, don't let that worry you ! " exclaimed Mr. Mosely ; " ef there's a strap or band about it, I'll pack it as easily as if it were a grip-sack. Let's have it at once ! "

Thus urged, Bruce stepped quickly into the house, returning with the instrument enveloped in a green-baize case.

" They'll take me for a traveling minstrel show, this time, sure enough," laughed Ike, passing the attached ribbon deftly over his shoulder.

" Rather a dangerous one to interfere with, though," commented Mrs. Kernochan, with a gesture indicative of his revolvers, contrasting strangely with the suggestion of the troubadour at his back.

" They don't tally very well together, thet's a fact ! " said Ike, glancing down, "but I'm equally prepared now, you see, for peace or war.—Well, good-by, ladies ; I must be off. It's a long ride yet to Oskaloo.—Come, boys ! " and, baring his bald brows in a sweeping salutation, the sheriff was off to the gate with his quick, nervous stride.

Jake Sharp and Humly Jim dropped down from the railing of the veranda, like a pair of rusty-coated crows which had been spending the interval in quiet and gloomy communion upon some convenient fence. With bows, that were phenomenal for their awkward originality, they slouched away after their chief.

There was a leisurely adjusting of girth and stir-rup at the rancho-gate, a hurried scramble into the saddle, and an abrupt departure. "Smithareens," developing some eccentricity—possibly owing to the strange burden her rider bore—called for a display of horsemanship on the part of the sheriff, which was promptly responded to with whip and spur. This incident awoke the latent humor and merriment of the two deputies. At last, with loud laughter, a clat-ter of hoofs, and an accompanying cloud of dust, the cavalcade got fairly under way. In a few moments their mounted figures were scarcely discernible amid the lengthening shadows of the valley.

9

THE gracious spring-time lingered lovingly in the valley of the Colorado. Nowhere had its advent been more welcome, nowhere more apparent its transforming changes. Amid weeks of brilliant sunlight, and odorous breezes, and the tuneful improvising of mating mocking-birds, the glad days came and went. From twilight to twilight the sun smiled benignly down from out the cloudless blue, and the earth, tropical with flowers and verdure, accepted gratefully his benediction. It was early in May. The year's resurrection was complete. The prairie-dogs bestirred themselves merrily about their noisy housekeeping, and chid the jocund season with their shrill clamor. And even the dismal violin-playing of the elder Dallas seemed to thrill at times with accents of joy.

The old man passed much of his time now in the open air, attired in that easy *negligé*, which became absolutely reckless as the season advanced. Coats and vests were cheerfully discarded, and even hats and boots. Neck-cloth and shirt-collar would have been renounced quite as willingly, had not these restraints of civilization always been abandoned as superfluous. The elder Dallas was apparently affected in warm weather by an impulse, similar to that which prompts the serpent to cast his skin. It had even been remarked by the editor of the "Oskaloo Criterion"—a local satirist, who spent a week in recruiting from his journalistic labors at the "Dallas Ranch" —that he "hadn't any use for a weather-indicator when 'All-sides' was in his neighborhood." He always "knew what kind of a day to expect from the alarming frankness of his costume at breakfast." This gentleman undoubtedly accepted the eccentricity of the old man's toilet in the light of a recording thermometer.

But, amid all the vagaries of Alcides's daily dress, his passion for his gloomy instrument was predominant. It was the inseparable companion of his walks and strolls—the sharer of his inactivity and revery. He would sit for hours beneath some dark live-oak, smiting the discords of his protesting fiddle, causing the sedate "Aulus" to lift eye and voice to heaven in piteous protest, and paralyzing the listening mockingbirds with the horror of his improvising. In divine despair they appeared to accept the impossibility of reproducing his achievements, and wondered and were still.

It was in his wanderings over his grassy range, however, that his musical efforts were most remarkable. While inspecting some of his sleek-skinned cattle, grazing in a fertile hollow, the impulse to perform would come upon him, and, sitting down upon a neighboring marmot-burrow, he would attempt some discordant inspiration, at which the prairie-dogs stood aghast, and the cattle bellowed their indignation ; concluding which, he would return to the ranch with an air of satisfaction worthy of a better cause. The crit-

ical observer might have argued from this musical
formality, a possible prelude to some approaching ceremony incident to the season ; but, since the elder
Dallas, as often as otherwise, went upon these pil-
grimages barefooted, it is possible the dismal concert
had its uses, for the considerate rattlesnakes respected
and spared this eccentric serpent-charmer.

But one day, as if in answer to the old man's in-
vocation, the "Dallas Range" awoke to life and animation.   Troops of cattle thundered through the
little valley, driven on by bands of horsemen, and
converging upon a large pen at its upper end.   The
air was full of the cries of lowing kine, the bleating
of calves, and the shouts of pursuing cow-boys.   The
plain was picturesque with the evolutions of the out-
riders, goading the terror-stricken bands, and throwing the unerring lasso.   The advance-guard of the
"spring round-ups" had reached the dwelling of the
elder Dallas.   The business of branding calves and
"cutting out" the various owners' property had begun.   In haste the aged cattle-owner discarded his
fiddle, resumed his knee-boots, and, mounting his
sturdy cow-pony, joined the boisterous cavalcade.

But the days passed drearily for Cynthia.   She
took no interest in the varied features of the round-
up.   The bursts of speed between the rival horsemen,
the exciting chase of some refractory steer, the skillful cast of the sinuous lariat, the shock and triumph
of each sharp encounter—scenes familiar to her, indeed, and in which she herself, mounted upon her
fleet little cow-pony, had often formed a conspicuous
figure, compelling the admiration of these centaurs
of the rein—these she witnessed with a listless eye or

did not regard at all. And, if the exciting chase interested her not, certainly still less the more prosaic details of throwing and branding the unfortunate calves, the cries of the tortured cattle, and the enumerating of the year's increase.

In all of these interesting particulars the elder Dallas manifested a keen delight, exhibiting a skill in horsemanship that those who were familiar with his usual rheumatic mode of progression could scarcely credit. He brought home with him to dinner, at odd times, certain of the "likeliest" of his companions—large-limbed, deep-chested sons of the saddle—introducing them to his charming daughter with a paternal flourish and hopeful manner that gave place to a mystified wonder, when he noted the apathy of Cynthia's greeting. He had anticipated no small degree of gratitude for the opportunity thus afforded of displaying her fascinations, and had congratulated himself in advance upon the havoc she would accomplish in a community where the very scarcity of the fair sex makes their advances irresistible.

But all these air-castles of the elder Dallas were doomed to speedy overthrow. To one and all Cynthia preserved a consistent attitude of calm indifference. The meal progressed in grave silence ; the infrequent conversation had no lighter topic than the incidents of the round-up ; and when, at its close, the admiring Alcides suggested—

"Ye might bring out yer banjo and shake it up for the boys a little ; show 'em jes' natch'ally what a stunner ye are at pickin' it "—this accomplished performer replied with an excuse, or instantly escaped to the seclusion of her own little room. Whereupon the embarrassed cow-men were compelled to endure an onslaught upon the violin that should have caused the embowering live-oaks to rise and mutiny.

But Cynthia went her way, and followed the dictates of her singular humor. "Aulus" and the fawn usually accompanied her in these lonely wanderings. Sometimes her listless footsteps sought the piny shelter of her bower, where, swinging in her little hammock, she passed long hours, steeped in the aromatic odors of the woods, watching the soft play of sunlight in the boughs above, her fancy captive and her thoughts adream. What secret she whispered in the ear of the sagacious hound that lay at her feet, meanwhile, his devoted eyes fixed ever upon her face; what thoughts of hers may have been detected by the antelope that drowsed away the long hours thus consecrated to her woodland reveries, have never been divulged by these most worthy confidantes. And if the grave pines, that bent so reverently about their little devotee, divined aught of her disquietude, they only grew the graver for the knowledge, and dropped a cone now and then in their still depths—a woodland tear of sympathy. And at such moments the river far below lifted a soft consolatory murmur that stole soothingly upon her silent musing.

For, I fear, our little Cynthia was but learning the story which, if we are to believe the poets, the vast panorama of Nature has been telling "since first the flight of years began." A sudden loneliness had come upon her in the midst of her pastimes and occupations. A strange voice whispered in her heart. The things which satisfied once had lost their charm somehow; the tones of her banjo were harsh and discordant ; the fawn had less of grace ; even her beloved "Aulus" was often stupid and unsatisfying.

At times the preoccupied Miss Dallas turned her footsteps in quite another direction. She developed a fascination for a certain ledge of rocks upon the crest of a western divide. It was a bare, uninterest-ing spot, without shade or shelter, and, but for the prospect it afforded of the valley on either side, a poor place certainly to pass one's time. Yet Cynthia was much given to haunting this locality. A superficial observer might have surmised that she sought this lofty post of observation, the more closely to note the varied manœuvres of the round-up in the plain below ; but, unfortunately for this theory, the back of the fair observer was invariably turned upon this animated spectacle. Who shall say what disappointments were hers, thus occupied in spying out the land ! Who shall say how many times this self-appointed Sister Anne beheld the cloud of dust upon the distant hori-zon disclose, not the expected horsemen, but the in-variable flock of sheep ! Or, how many times some roving mustang raised a tumultuous flutter in that little breast, that not a whole *caballada* of his wild-eyed comrades could have caused by the maddest of their onsets ! Yet even in this hopeless reconnoitring the days sped on and on, and the anticipated horse-man never came.

I must not omit to mention a certain formality in dress which Miss Dallas began to affect about this time. It was in the direction of long trains and trail-ing habits. There was much mysterious rehearsal in the seclusion of her little room, a disposition to gather her skirts in one gloved hand and tiptoe about, avoid-

ing intermediate objects with an acquired daintiness
and grace.   There were certain fastidious airs of
manner which were deftly caught and quite as faith-
fully rehearsed in private.   During these ceremonies
a small riding-whip, formerly presented to Cynthia
by Mr. Buck Jerrold, was generally carried lightly in
the right hand.   A swift canter over the adjacent
hills, attended by the same scrutiny of the remote
horizon, invariably followed this painstaking performance.

Such mysterious behavior was not without provok-
ing the comment of other members of the household.

"I should reckon yo' was practicin' fo' the tight-
rope, wi' all yo' airs and graces, Mis' Cynthy," the
ebony Amelia remonstrated.

"Is there any private theatricals goin' to come off
down at San Marcus?" inquired the mystified Alcides, having through the open door caught a glimpse
of his daughter attitudinizing.   "I didn't know,
from thet thar high-steppin', but you war posin' fur
the stony-hearted princess thet refuses the poor but
deservin' young man in the play."

To all this ingenious badinage Miss Dallas preserved an attitude of disdainful reticence.   But she
was manifestly unhappy and ill at ease.   That joyous,
light-hearted gayety which once possessed her had
taken wings.   She sang no more, where once her glad
voice challenged the mocking-bird.   She was as capricious as an April day.   Peevish and fretful with
her father for the most part, there were intervals of
sudden tenderness, when she overwhelmed him with
kisses and caresses.   Possibly, at such moments, a
certain absent individual was ever present to her fancy,

whose name she never suffered to pass her lips. Philosophers aver that, in matters of the heart, there is a species of cold comfort in thus lavishing the affections by proxy.

During this unsatisfactory period Cynthia's treatment of Mr. Buck Jerrold was most remarkable. This gentleman had been wont to visit her often, to pass hours in her society, to sit quietly by her side, silent and thoughtful, smoking his pipe, and noting her every word or action with a reverence and admiration that was little short of worship. Formerly Miss Dallas had permitted this oppressive homage as if hers by a species of divine right; had laughed and chatted with him pleasantly, accepted his little gifts and keepsakes gratefully, sent him upon her errands with the air of conferring a favor, and exerted her many fascinations in a way known only to the sex.

All this had been most agreeable to Jerrold. With evident satisfaction he basked in the sunshine of her favor. But a change came suddenly about. With the advent of the spring round-ups came more frequent visits on the part of that gentleman, and a strange waywardness in Cynthia's reception. She greeted him with marked embarrassment and restraint. The former silence of his manner was now eclipsed by her own taciturnity. Jerrold was often astounded at his eloquence in his efforts to entertain her, but Cynthia was at all times absent and distraught, and appeared to be haunted by a nervous dread that Mr. Jerrold was about to say something which it would give her great pain to hear. Upon the slightest pretext she would escape him, and bury herself amid the solitudes of the sympathetic pines.

Here that strange trouble which made her heart ache would occasionally overflow her eyes, and there were tears shed in the dim woods as little bidden as understood—tears which the pines bemoaned and the bluebirds and squirrels held sacred, but which somehow brought the balm of relief to her who shed them.

I do not think, through it all, that Miss Dallas was really conscious of being in love ; only in a general way that she was bereaved and disappointed. The occurrences of the past few months had come to her in the light of a revelation. She was suddenly aware of the existence of some one who possessed for her a peculiar sympathy, whose words awoke a responsive echo in her heart—some one immeasurably superior to the rough men she usually encountered. She could not explain the strange claim this hitherto unrealized nature had upon her ; she only knew that it existed ; that she longed for its influence ; that she grieved when it was denied. And there was associated with this feeling, as there always is, one of pique and injury for the apparent neglect which she had suffered.

How much this state of mind was alleviated when the obliging sheriff put into her hands the guitar sent by Henry Bruce it is impossible to say. Certain it is that never instrument was the recipient of more tender treatment. She adorned it with ribbons, carried it about with her constantly, and practiced assiduously upon it. About this time the elder Dallas, recognizing a formidable rival, abandoned his own exertions upon the violin. He viewed the advent of the guitar with suspicion, and commented upon it with cynicism. Apparently he recognized, in the soft harmonies Cynthia's deft fingers struck from the strings, a dangerous ally to sentiment. Alcides, as we have seen, was a foe to romance.

"Ye wanter look out, Cynthy, fur the poetry and nonsense thet thar tarnal thing 'll fill you chuck full of, ef ye once turn it loose on yer onguarded feelin's," he said, gravely, surprising her once playing upon it with eyes that were wistful and far away. "It's a destroyer of the appetite, and gener'ly plumb full o' onsatisfactoriness," bestowing a glance upon the glistening strings that was full of foreboding. "I knew a girl once thet was thet led away by one of them jinglin' critters thet she didn't do nothin' else but play an' lie 'round, a-longin' and a-yearnin', until by-and-by the sallow-faced critter got herself clean bewitched. Her family and friends could do nothin' with her; she wouldn't eat nothin'; and fin'ly she went into a gallopin' consumption, and they buried her one very damp day in the arly spring."

But, in spite of this terrible example of the fascination of guitar-playing, Cynthia still persisted in her practicing. She endured with cheerfulness the sore fingers, tired wrists, and other annoyances which this exacting instrument imposes upon its devotees. And she received no end of encouragement in other ways. The mocking-birds which fled aghast from the shrieking violin sometimes favored her with imitative outbursts—that sincerest form of flattery. Perched on some tossing spray, or flickering here and there in their odd "half-mourning," they reproduced snatches of her waltzes and fandangos. There was a certain sentimental lizard with a speculative eye that would bask daily upon a sunny rock, and from his rapt demeanor during her performance, was apparently en-

abled to obtain glimpses of the infinite, hitherto
denied. And "Aulus" sympathized, and without remonstrance lent his quiet and dignified approval.
And the fawn was soothed into that dreamy languor
that was fast becoming habitual.

So the days passed ; and Cynthia's heart found
much of consolation, and Mr. Buck Jerrold wondered
at the change in his dulcinea, and had long confer-
ences with the mystified Alcides, who was annoyed
and fretful, and made mysterious reference to the
prevalence of malaria and the existence of "dumb
ager"—the inference being that his lovely daughter
was suffering from the maladies of a forward spring.
Until one day Mr. Jerrold surprised the old man with
this query :

"Ye don't reckon, then, thet the visit of thet thar
Henry Bruce hez hed anythin' to do with this yer
change ?   It's *my* opinion thet's what's done it."

"Why, he wa' n't here more'n two days at the
furthest," remonstrated the father, staring at his ques-
tioner.

"Thet's all right," returned Jerrold, meditatively,
"but it don't take any great length of time with the
proper person.   I've been told thar's been cases where
it was only a word or a look thet done the biz'ness.
Purvided thet's the true state of the case," he added,
stretching his huge limbs awkwardly, while a weary
look crept suddenly into his eyes—"purvided thet's
it, and he proves himself to be a better man nur I
am, Cynthy must take her ch'ice.   I hevn't got nothin' ag'in him ; he's a square sort of chap, and a man,
ez *is* a man, can stand bein' beat by a straightforrard
feller who is better fixed and better favored."

Then came a letter from Henry Bruce to Cynthia, couched in delicate terms, wherein he expressed regret that he was unable to act as her escort to the coming ball at San Marcus, but that courtesy necessitated that he should accompany Miss Stafford. Cynthia perused this missive calmly, wept over it in private, and then acted with the perverseness of womankind. She did not change her attitude toward the deserving Mr. Jerrold, but she sat down and indited a long epistle to the neglectful and dangerous Captain Foraker, in which she reproached that gentleman for his long absence from her side, represented herself as languishing from lack of his attentions, and inquired if he could spare time from his engrossing military duties to take her to the coming festivity. And Captain Foraker, vain, critical, and complacent, read this letter carefully over his after-dinner cigar, smiled superciliously, adjusted his officer's cap rakishly over his distracting curls, and, mounting his horse, rode over from the Post, and passed the afternoon with Cynthia.

That he was received with a cordiality he had no reason nor right to expect; that Cynthia flirted with him desperately, and in a manner calculated to strike despair into the heart of Buck Jerrold; and that the irate Alcides was moved several times, in the course of that eventful afternoon, to cast longing glances in the direction of the "Silent Mary," may be readily imagined by the reader who has remarked the inconsistency of woman when dominated by pique.

Small wonder that Captain Foraker promised to go to the ball; that he listened cheerfully to Cynthia's plan to visit Miss Bertha Maverick, the fascinating daughter of the village blacksmith, and agreed to call for her at that lady's home on the evening in question ; and that he rode back to his quarters with a self-satisfied smile upon his supercilious features, curling his gray mustache, and otherwise pluming himself upon the triumphs of the afternoon. That, after his departure, Cynthia dismissed him utterly from her mind ; that, beyond the satisfaction of having averted the awful possibility of being a "wall-flower" at the San Marcus ball, she experienced nothing but regret ; that she realized herself the vanity and unprofitableness of all earthly things, while she succeeded in filling the minds of Jerrold and Dallas with solicitude ; and that she hated Miss Stafford cordially, and was conscious, in her heart of hearts, that Henry Bruce was more fascinating than ever—are facts that will readily occur to her appreciative and discriminating sex, to whose tender sympathies her present emotions are intrusted.

X

For weeks it had been apparent at San Marcus that a social event of unusual importance was impending. For weeks a flutter of expectancy had disquieted the feminine heart, displaying itself in animated gossip upon the street corners, in an alarming tendency to indulge in afternoon calls, and a reckless patronage of seamstress and milliner. The affable clerks at Murray's store had the tedious hours of business enlivened by coy visits from local belles, nervously fussy about the fit of high-heeled kid boots, and painfully fastidious in regard to the cut of a glove or the tint of a ribbon. They beset the shop-counters in trios and pairs, and quite demoralized the perspiring store-keeper. There was much promenading in the single business street of the little village, indulged in so aimlessly as to give the observer the general impression of a rehearsal. But it was apparent that feminine curiosity culminated at the river, whither, over the level plain, the main thoroughfare of San Marcus led, and to which locality the footsteps of the fair daughters were most persistently directed.

Foremost among these lovely pedestrians was Miss Bertha Maverick, with an eye like the flash of a bayonet, and a profile decidedly aquiline. She could be seen on any pleasant afternoon, defying the admiration of the baffled sun with a parasol of pale pink, and leading on, as it were, by this oriflamme of sentiment, the thronging cohorts of Texan coquetry. Three days of aimless pilgrimaging on the part of the San Marcus maidens, and all at once was seen the method of this vernal madness. Occasional horsemen began to be met with on the dusty highway. By degrees the number of these was augmented to mounted squads and groups, until at last their proportions reached those of an occasional cavalcade. Of course, this irruption of eligible manhood was the occasion of much indiscriminate flirtation, and there were many glances given and exchanged that boded ill for the future peace of mind of the parties concerned. Mischievous eyes challenged observation beneath dainty bonnets, and the tilted sun-shade was eloquent of the warfare of Cupid. Need it be said that bronzed and bearded faces accepted these overtures with more than equal frankness, that the fluttering handkerchief in every instance received the recognition of the raised sombrero, and that everywhere along this dangerously active highway there was a disposition on the part of either sex to halt frequently and look back ?

But, once in town, these amorous advances of the sterner sex gave rise to reckless outlay of capital and a remarkable solicitude in matters of dress. The barber was put into requisition, and the demand for "b'iled shirts" and "store-clothes" threatened to exceed the limited supply of those articles. Although the proprietor of the Half-way House had made unusual preparation for this influx of custom, and had taken the precaution to prepare the unfurnished bedrooms upon the upper corridor for occupancy, it was soon found necessary on the part of guests to "double up," and, in many instances, the floor and even the roof were utilized, on account of the extensive opportunities they afforded for sleeping purposes. It was whispered that the two Ludeling brothers—great gallants of the Southwest—despairing of accommodation at the village hostelry, had been obliged to pass the night in the rear of the saloon, camping out with blanket and saddle in true frontier fashion. That the hard counters of Murray's store afforded restless slumbers to a portion of this excessive population was a matter of common report. The outcome of all this was to strengthen the popular impression that the "Half-way House" had been well christened.

Perhaps it was for these reasons that the visitors devoted little of their time to slumber. Business was brisk in the gambling-saloons and bar-rooms. The pop of the lager-beer cork responded to the click of the billiard-ball, and there was a large gathering of men about the "monte-game" of a local blackleg, and the usual instructive interchange of cash and experience.

Meanwhile, notes in very erratic handwriting were constantly flying about. Mr. Lariat, in conformance with a custom as absurd as unnecessary, was giving Miss Lone Star preliminary notice that he contemplated the pleasure of calling upon her ; and the latter lady was responding that she would take pleasure in being at home in anticipation of that gratifying event. And so feminine vanity was flattered on the one hand, and the manly breast disquieted for some days to come on the other, by these rare opportunities for visiting ; the dearth of womanhood upon the frontier

10

rendering young manhood practically defenseless. And, to facilitate this dangerous state of things, the event of the ball approached, at which music and the dance—those destroyers of philosophy—were to finish matters and put the *coup de grâce* to the general infatuation.

Through the foresight of Bruce and Kernochan, the best room in the "Half-way House" had been engaged in advance for Kate and Edith. For themselves the gentlemen accepted with good humor such primitive quarters as opportunity afforded. On the morning of the eventful day, they drove down to San Marcus in a light conveyance, reaching the little hostelry in time for dinner. Here they registered in the small blank-book which answered for the usual hotel register, and Miss Stafford noted, with some merriment, that an entry made by Phil Kernochan on Christmas-day, two years previous, occurred only four pages back. Here that lady's patrician nostrils were saluted with the odor of kerosene and frontier cookery, and, after enduring the stuffy atmosphere and rheumatic appointments of her bedroom, she came down to dinner with an amusement very similar to that with which luxurious people enter upon the enjoyment of a picnic.

Doubtless by the time she had discussed this remarkable meal, eaten amid promiscuous society, and overseered by the officious proprietor—who kept up a running fire of conversation with the myrmidons of the kitchen through a long slit in the wainscot, and dealt his plates and appetizing dishes over the heads of his guests with great recklessness and liberality— the novelty of Texan hotel-life began to pall somewhat upon the young lady. I can not say that Edith's appetite was improved, either by the panoramic view of hotel cookery the wainscot afforded, or by the gentleman opposite, who ate molasses on his pie, and supplied a very wide mouth with a very large knife, and a general suggestion that the unnatural size of the aperture was due to the hazard attending this experiment. Howbeit, the meal was endured, and perhaps in dread of dyspeptic retribution, Miss Stafford proposed to Henry Bruce to take her for a short stroll through the town. To this the gentleman readily assented, and passing the long line of vicious and kicking saddle-horses, tethered in front of the hotel, they joined the animated procession of strollers that idled through the main street of San Marcus.

I leave to the imagination how much attention the fair Northerner attracted, what admiring glances from under broad sombreros were cast after her erect figure and graceful carriage, and with what envious whispers of detraction the belles of the village remarked the faultnessness of her fashionable walking-dress. But I must mention one incident of this afternoon walk. They had reached a point about half-way between the hotel and the river, when a familiar voice caused Bruce to raise his eyes. Cynthia stood before him, looking very pretty and engaging from the becoming depths of a quaint poke-bonnet. She was accompanied by an elderly man in the dress of an officer. He was nonchalantly puffing a cigar. Miss Bertha Maverick, escorted by a cow-man of athletic build and awkward gait, was just behind her.

A quick color mounted to Cynthia's cheek, and she bowed hurriedly to Bruce, as she raised her eyes with a smile of coquetry to the man at her side. A rapid interchange of hostilities passed between the ladies in a discriminating survey of one another's costumes, which was more expressive than words. Miss Bertha Maverick, with supercilious eyelids and defiant nostrils, re-enforced her less aggressive companion. Bruce, who was about to speak, noting at once the armed neutrality of all parties, raised his hat and passed on. But, as he did so, he heard Miss Bertha Maverick remark in a high, metallic voice :

"'Thet's the stuck-up piece you was tellin' me about—eh, Cynthia? Well, ef I reckoned I was so powerful fascinatin', I wouldn't let every one know it whenever I met 'em. The airs and graces of thet fast-colored brunette is enough to natch'ally paralyze an eight-day kitchen-clock."

The dull red globe of the setting sun went down that afternoon in mortification, blushing itself to death before the silver glories of the splendid moon that rose full-orbed and queenly over the San Marcus hills. A crimson glow lingered along the horizon where the shame of day's discomfiture was shared by a few sympathetic clouds. An occasional planet, serene and pulseless, hung poised in the limitless ether and graced the triumphant destinies of night; but the thousand lesser stars were lost in the rare effulgence of the dominant moon.

With the first shadows of evening, public curiosity began to be attracted in the direction of a long, low structure, whose spacious outlines and shutterless windows showed black against the lighter sky.

This building had been reared in the interests of

Erin by a prosperous Hibernian, who rejoiced in the classic name of Ulysses Magindy, and consecrated his architectural efforts and poetic memories under the title of "Tara's Hall." But the cynical Texan youth were wanting in reverence for Ireland's legendary past. "Tarrier's Hall" was the popular rendering of Mr. Magindy's poetic christening. Actuated by the same spirit of skepticism, they pelted the edifice with mud and stones, and sent vagrant tomato-cans on voyages of discovery through its ancient lights. Externally, it was a pathetic diagram of its owner's highly lacerated feelings.

But there were occasions when the importance of "Tarrier's Hall" impressed itself even upon this derisive public. During political meetings, religious revivals, and temperance crusades, the hand of the vandal was stayed. Among such intervals of immunity was the present. The very rabble that had been most active in bombardment now bestowed themselves in attempted renovation and repair. The spacious auditorium was swept and aired ; the relics of barbarism were removed ; the draughts from the windows effectually sealed by the intervention of card-board, bits of carpet, and cast-off hats ; and even the redeeming touches of putty and varnish were here and there attempted.

And when feminine taste was added to the rude but practical efforts of men, it was wonderful to note the transforming change ; to see how the ravages of time and abuse yielded to a little well-bestowed decoration. On this occasion the San Marcus maidens had employed the garniture of hemlock-boughs and gayly colored muslin with telling effect, and the tallow-candles perched everywhere seemed to threaten a general conflagration.

Mr. Ulysses Magindy, himself, was at present going about the building and lighting these candles with a long pole, attended by a gang of small boys, who restrained their uncomplimentary epithets in view of the coming festivity. And scarcely had the last elevated dip commenced to contribute its greasy droppings to the gratuitous shower that rained everywhere upon the ball-room floor, when, with laughter and merriment, the guests began to arrive and take up their positions on the hard wooden benches that were ranged at either end of the room.

Of course, an occasion so celebrated as this crowning event of the frontier season had attracted the widely scattered beauty of the region. The affair was graced by the contributory fascinations of outlying towns. Miss Cordelia Delancey—the "Wild Rose of San Saba"—the perfume of whose attractions had been already blown abroad by the prairie breezes as far east as San Marcus, was present to blossom anew, and to excite even more fragrant fancies in the minds of her poetic admirers. Miss Flo' Brooks, clear-eyed and bewitching, held out alluringly the fascinations of her native town of Paint Rock. There were other humbler importations, against whose staid mediocrity these celebrated beauties flashed as against a somber background. The local honors were sustained by Miss Bertha Maverick and Miss Cynthia Dallas.

But public interest in the San Marcus ball was better shown in the attendance of the men. There was a generous sprinkling of frontier celebrities. Mr. Joe Treddle was on hand, generously disguised in liquor, having accomplished the great feat of riding from San Marcus to San Saba on his bicycle—a distance of over two hundred miles—and finding it necessary to stimulate freely to overcome fatigue after the exploit. "Kickapoo Dick" lent the occasion his frontier playfulness and humor. Mr. Josh Blunt was present, the truculent but unswerving satellite of Miss Flo' Brooks. Captain Jack Foraker, conspicuous among the bearded cow-boys for his military bearing and complacent curling of his gray mustache, was devoted to Cynthia, but generally observant of the fair ones, as if he were under the impression that he was giving the ladies a treat. And the elder Dallas, morbidly alive to the fact that Foraker was his daughter's escort, had placed the "Silent Mary" and his violin in his shaky carry-all, driven down to San Marcus, and put in an early appearance on the scene of action. Stowing the heavy goose-gun carefully away behind the ball-room door, so that it might be available in case of emergency, he entered "Tarrier's Hall" with his trusty fiddle in a green-baize bag beneath his arm, and an eye biliously observant of the festive scene. Not that he really had any intention of playing at the *fête*, but that, in his nervous anxiety for his daughter's society, he took it along with him from a sense of loneliness and sympathy, and perhaps, too, from force of habit.

A certain aged violinist, renowned on the frontier for his music and erratic evolutions upon the floor while playing, had already opened the ball. The waltz, tortured by cow-boy enthusiasts into something between a can-can and a Dutch "*spiel*," was exciting the laughter of Edith Stafford and Henry Bruce.

"You see some strange steps here," remarked that gentleman to Judge Natchez, who was present. "At least, they strike *me* as strange from their novelty; but I suppose you have become used to them."

"Not at all," replied his Honor, smiling—the gentleman was descended from one of the first families of Virginia—"not at all, sir; I have passed a good twenty years on the frontier, but there are some steps taken here to-night which I think I can safely say I never expect to get used to."

"*Ab uno disce omnia*," and I say no more of the grotesque evolutions cut that night by slippered and booted feet. If Miss Stafford laughed, it was guardedly, for she feared to give offense, and, whenever she could, she disguised the cause of her merriment by glancing at the fiddler, who collided with the dancers, and coruscated about the ball-room like a musical rocket.

But, at one time, gravity was out of the question. It was when Alcides Dallas—who had stood aloof in a corner of the room, regarding the proceedings with malevolence and ill-favor—all at once selected a large chair, and, placing it gravely in the center of the floor, seated himself with a deliberation that was unmistakable. Here he removed his violin from the green-baize bag, and, without stopping to tune it, entered into hearty and heart-breaking rivalry of the regular musician.

No pen can describe the order of dancing from that moment. The waltzing continued, interspersed by frequent lanciers and quadrilles, but, from the time that Alcides began to support the local fiddler, the muse of melody fled the scene.

"Isn't the floor just lovely ?" remarked Miss Bertha Maverick to her escort, after an intoxicating whirl in the effort to keep time to the music.

"Yes," returned Mr. Ludeling, "the floor is well enough, but the orchestra paralyzes me altogether ; let us walk out upon the gallery, and get a chance to think."

And, indeed, the more philosophical, and those apparently beyond the influence of sound, followed the suggestion. Even "Lampasas Jake," who was stone-deaf, was seen to leave the room abruptly. How far the rumor, that the proprietor of the Half-way House had broached a barrel of rye-whisky in the neighboring wagon-shed, may have influenced this sudden exodus, is a matter of conjecture. Certain it is that many of those who left returned with a peculiar light about the eye and a disposition to friskiness in deportment. From this time forward it was no rarity to see men waltzing together, and deriving no end of satisfaction from the entertainment. There was also a tendency, on the part of certain solitary dancers, to seek some quiet corner of the ball-room, and sing softly to themselves, with that enjoyment which only alcohol can inspire. It may have been that the sudden outbreak of the elder Dallas was contagious ; but, be that as it may, his action, at least, afforded Edith the pretext she required, for scarcely had the violin duet begun, when she was asked to dance by Mr. Buck Jerrold. Here was a quandary. The high-born Northerner hardly cared to extend this privilege to Mr. Jerrold, but she did not wish to hurt his feelings, in view of his gallant behavior in her late predicament. So she fell back in condemnation of the orchestra.

"Really, Mr. Jerrold," she said, smiling sweetly
up into his face, "I could not dance one step to such
time as those fiddles are playing. I have just refused
Mr. Bruce here. Shall we not walk upon the porch?"
And with this pretext she left the room on the arm
of her deliverer.

Bruce, abandoned thus to himself, found the time
drag wearily. He was not edified by Cynthia's behavior with Captain Foraker. Beyond a mere slight
recognition, little conversation had passed between
them. But throughout the evening she flirted with
the officer desperately, and with an ostentation that
irritated Bruce. The captain accepted his fair companion's advances complacently. He waltzed a great
deal, and, it was noticeable, left the ball-room at the
end of every dance. By degrees the effect of these
frequent trips began to be apparent in his manner and
gestures. He did not confine his attentions to Cynthia, but was mildly playful and familiar with the
other ladies. Miss Dallas appeared a little annoyed
at this, but attempted to disguise it in conversation
with Miss Maverick and her escort.

At last, during one of his most genial moments,
Captain Foraker crossed the ball-room unsteadily to
the place where Edith was sitting. She had returned,
and was chatting with Mr. Jerrold. The Captain
posed himself engagingly before Miss Stafford, and,
without the formality of an introduction, requested
the favor of the next dance. Miss Stafford raised her
brown eyes in surprise, regarded the Captain a moment, and then turned coldly away. Temporarily
disconcerted, the gentleman described a half circle to
the left, and coming back to the same point repeated

his request. His gray mustache, elevated at an inebriated angle, gave his countenance a droll expression.

"I de-shire favor of-f w-waltsh," repeated the captain, in a very high key.

This was too much for Henry Bruce. The blood rushed to his face as he rose to his feet.

"You forget yourself, sir!" he said, sternly—"the lady is not dancing, and, if she were, you are not in a condition to remember your etiquette."

Captain Foraker gazed at Bruce in a dazed way. It was a ludicrous but critical moment. The next a blow might have been struck and a scene followed. The moment passed. An imbecile smile spread itself over his puffed face, as if the humor of his predicament asserted itself in spite of his drunken discomfiture. He turned on his heel and returned to his position at the opposite end of the room.

A diversion was here afforded by the entrance of a singular figure. He was a tall, lean, cadaverous man with long, jet-black hair, straggling beard, low brows, and piercing black eyes. He strolled into the room with an impudent swagger, his slouch hat on the back of his head, his hands in his pockets, and his pantaloons tucked into his boots. In neglecting other details of his toilet he had also omitted his ablutions, and his general appearance was disordered and unsavory. But none of these facts apparently contributed to the general sensation at his entrance. The ladies stared; the men scowled; some swore and others laughed; an audible murmur of astonishment went round the room. But the effect upon Alcides was most peculiar. It put an instant stop to his music. He set down bow and fiddle and rose with nervous haste. After regarding the intruder a second with a glance in which rage and surprise struggled for the mastery, he took a few hasty steps in the direction of the "Silent Mary," apparently thought better of his resolve, came back, and, sweeping chair, violin, and bow before him, seated himself against the opposite wall, tilting back and plunging his hands deep in his pockets with an expression of amazed resignation. In this position he remained, apparently uncertain what he should do next.

Meanwhile, the uncleanly individual, after looking boldly about the room, sauntered over to a corner where certain of the uninvited guests were standing, polluting the atmosphere of the ball-room with cheap cigars, and generally absorbed in the incidents of the evening. The manner in which the new-comer was received by this group was in no sense flattering. No one offered a word of greeting or even a sign of recognition. Apparently, the entrance of Mr. Lemuel Wickson, the horse-thief, upon the San Marcus festivities was regarded as an intrusion.

There was a sudden stir near the door, and Sheriff Mosely entered. He strode to the center of the ball-room with his quick, nervous stride, and cast a sharp glance in every direction. He was armed, and his manner was significant. For a second he stood quiet, his small figure rigid, his alert eyes glancing about. The next he espied Lemuel Wickson, and, with a hurried gesture to his belt, he sprang forward.

A rush in that quarter on the part of the men immediately followed. The ladies huddled together—a frightened bevy—at the upper end of the room.

Lem Wickson awaited the approach of Sheriff
Mosely with composure. Beyond the slipping of his
right hand carelessly beneath his coat, he did not
change his attitude. The sheriff did not stop until
he reached that quarter of the room, when, halting
suddenly, the formality of a surly nod was exchanged.

"Time's up, Lem," remarked Ike, coolly. "I
want you."

"What for?" demanded Mr. Wickson, gruffly,
without moving a muscle.

"In partickler, on a warrant sworn ag'in you for
horse-stealin' by Alcides Dallas and Buck Jerrold,"
replied Mr. Mosely, "but it orter happened some time
ago for hog-stealin' and gin'ral cussedness."

"Not this evenin', Ike," replied Lem, incredulously, leaning against the wall and allowing one hand
to rest carelessly on his hip. "I reckon to put in
my time at this hyar ball to-night—dance with the
gals, and enjoy myself gin'rally."

"Oh, ye do?" said the sheriff, his blue eyes taking on a sudden, hard glitter; "well, I don't reckon
thet little diversion to take place, if thar's any law in
the Lone Star. Wot's more, I'm the man to prevent it."

He made a quick dash at his belt and a sudden
spring forward. There was a rush and a scuffle, during which the figures of both men whirled before the
eyes of the spectators. A second later Lem Wickson held the sheriff by the throat, his right hand
leveling upon him a large "Smith and Wesson."

The sheriff struggled frantically in his gripe, his
hand plucking at his revolver, which appeared to be
caught. It was a perilous moment. The rough men

looking on held their breath. It chanced that Henry Bruce was nearest to Wickson—the brandished weapon at full-cock within the reach of his arm. With a sudden dart forward he grasped the horse thief's wrist with his left hand, and, seizing the "barrel-catch" between the finger and thumb of his right, by a quick, strong pull unshipped the barrel, throwing the cartridges all over the room.

It was an act sublime in its desperation and the skill of its achievement. It showed, moreover, a re-remarkable knowledge of the weapon. In a twinkling Bruce had closed with the disarmed and astounded ruffian, and pinning him against the opposite wall, released the sheriff.

"Well done!" gasped the nearly throttled Ike, glancing admiringly upon Bruce. He took a pair of handcuffs from his pocket, and by a quick movement secured his prisoner. Then he turned upon the breathless crowd.

"I don't mind sayin' right here, thet thet's about the neatest trick I ever yet seen done, and ef Lem thar hed hed a 'Colt's,' my life wouldn't been worth a pecan. Dog-gone this old greasy belt!" he exclaimed, glancing down where his revolver had slipped beyond the hammer in the worn leather, thereby making it difficult to draw—"dog-gone it! I hev hed trouble with thet holster afore, and now it nearly closed my record. I reckon I'd better make a requisition for a new belt."

"Give us yer hand, pardner," he said again, turning once more to Henry Bruce. "It does Ike Mosely good to feel the grip of a good man and true. If yer ever wantin' anythin' very bad, or needin' any help,

I reckon ye know whar you kin get it arter to-night. Ye kin count on the Sheriff of Oskaloo, any time, and ez often ez you want to, for the last drop o' his blood. I don't know on the whole," he added, with a sudden change of manner, "but what I might as well cement that statement with a practical snifter."

He took a flask of whisky from his pocket and extended it to Bruce.

The latter declined courteously.

"Jes' ez you say," remarked Ike, quietly, "but yer not actin' ez sensible ez ye did a minute ago, and yer losin' a chance to sp'ile some mighty good liquor. I sampled this myself."

"Well," he said, pausing to take breath before testing the qualities of his flask, "here's the health of a man the county is proud of. I'm lookin' at ye, pardner, along with the rest of the town of Oskaloo."

He raised the flask to his lips and tossed off a draught with an accompanying smack. With characteristic good-will he turned immediately to Wickson.

"No hard feelin's, Lem," he said, generously, "seein' the late onpleasantness is over. Ef yer feelin' like tryin' this stuff, I don't mind holdin' it fur ye to git the benefit."

He extended the flask good-humoredly to the latter's lips. But Mr. Wickson was not in the humor for whisky, and signified it by turning impatiently away.

"All right," said Ike, restoring the flask to his pocket, without pressing his hospitality further upon the thronging crowd, a few of whom wore an expression which made it evident that refusal was extremely unlikely.

"It's a sing'lar thing, sometimes, how good licker goes beggin'. Not thet it often occurs here in Texas, but thet, when it does, it's worth while to take note of it. I disremember any such depressin' state of facts, sence I felt called upon to invent thet 'temperance mead' for the ball over at Brady.—Good-evenin', gentlemen. I trust I heven't materially interfered with the festivities."

He turned on his heel, and, with his hand on the arm of his prisoner, left the ball-room.

Of course so exciting an occurrence as the recent arrest, was not without its effect upon the general gayety. After the sheriff's departure, it was a difficult matter to get the frightened ladies in the humor to resume dancing. Possibly this difficulty was materially increased by the fact that the fiddler was not to be found, but was at last discovered asleep in an old carry-all in the shed, hard by the whisky-cask already alluded to, and with a glass of spirits in his hand. His violin had fallen from his grasp during his recent alcoholic weakness, and had been crushed by the boot-heel of some other follower of Bacchus.

No one dared think of the elder Dallas in this emergency, but he, too, had fled the ball-room. Under these discouraging circumstances the ladies lingered a little, chatting with their escorts, and by-and-by began to go home.

Edith and Henry Bruce remained long enough to see certain patrons of the whisky-keg enter upon an entertaining pastime. Having discovered that the drippings from the candles were now pretty evenly distributed by the recent dancing, some genius attempted to improvise a slide. The idea became

speedily popular, and soon a long line of boisterous
revelers were joined in this ambitious effort to trans-
form the ball-room into a skating-rink. The edify-
ing diversion was continued until a late hour of the
evening.

The clear, round moon rode high and shone deeply
down when Bruce and Edith departed. As they did
so, the former caught a glimpse of a figure, skulking
along beneath the bright light, and carrying a heavy
gun. It was Alcides Dallas.

The singular movements of the old man awakened
his curiosity, and his eye mechanically followed him
as he moved up the road. He appeared to be following some one and suspiciously noting his movements.
Glancing ahead, Bruce beheld in one of the moonlit
spaces of the level road the figures of Cynthia and
Captain Foraker proceeding slowly. Miss Bertha
Maverick and the younger Mr. Ludeling were some
distance behind. The captain was walking unsteadily,
and discussing some question in a decidedly loud tone
of voice ; Cynthia was endeavoring to quiet him.

Bruce could not repress a smile, as he realized that
the entire party were unconsciously under the armed
surveillance of the suspicious Alcides. But, though
in a measure amused, he did not direct the attention
of the fastidious young lady at his side to the humor
of the incident. During the walk home he conversed
but little, being occupied with his reflections. At
length, when they arrived at the Half-way House, he
surprised Miss Stafford with the information that he
intended taking a short ride or walk before retir-
ing.

"At this hour of the night ?" exclaimed Edith,

11

who was a trifle piqued by his recent abstraction. "I should think, Hal, you were absolutely daft."

"Not in the least ; only bored with the noise and excitement of that pandemonium," Bruce replied, as they passed up the broad steps of the veranda.

He bade her good-night in the hallway, and turned away, leaving her gazing curiously after him as he went out again into the moonlight.

XI

HENRY BRUCE walked rapidly away in the mellow light of the moon. By the side of a leprous sycamore he paused to light a cigar. In the quick, upspringing light of the match he beheld a man, seated upon the door-stone of Murray's store and dejectedly smoking. The soft moon-rays beat gently down upon the dejected figure, idealizing his attitude. The man was armed, and his revolvers glanced in the moonlight. A large, rawboned horse stood gauntly outlined in the shadow. Bruce recognized Buck Jerrold and the erratic "Buckshot."

"A fine night for a ride," he said, puffing his cigar.

Mr. Jerrold raised his head gloomily.

"Well enough for them ez cares to ride," he assented, "but I ain't in no humor fer thet sort of amusement."

"Tastes differ," replied Bruce, pleasantly, noting the other's manner, and shrewdly divining its cause. "Now, I should like nothing better—myself."

"Why don't ye start in then?" returned Mr. Jerrold; "I'm sure thar's prairie enough before ye to make it an object."

"Simply because I have no horse," Bruce re-

joined. "I came over from the ranch with the rest
of my party in a carriage."

"Wal, ef thet's all thet stands in yer way," replied
the accommodating Mr. Jerrold, taking his pipe from
his lips, "thar's 'Buckshot.' Barrin' a disposition to
rare and 'buck' now and then, ez ye've seen, he's a
peart hoss enough, and is at your service. For myself,
I've got enough to think about, without ridin' into
the bargain."

He took a six-shooter from his belt and regarded
it absently, cocking and uncocking the weapon with
the finger and thumb of his brawny right hand. The
clicking of the lock sounded ominously in the still
night.

Bruce looked curiously at the man before availing
himself of his offer. He seemed to have something
upon his mind. However, he untethered "Buckshot," and hanging the long riata from the saddle-
bow, sprang into the saddle.

"Where shall I find you, to return your horse?"
he inquired.

"Oh, anywhere," Mr. Jerrold replied, indifferently. "Hitch him where you like in town, or leave
him at the 'Two Brothers.' I'm sure to find him."

"All right," replied Bruce, dashing away.

He rode at a swinging gallop through the main
street of the little frontier town, the hoofs of his
horse echoing loudly on the level road. In a few
moments he had left the settlement behind him and
was alone upon the vast, illimitable plain.

The grateful transition from the feverish scene he
had recently quitted to the perfect freedom of boundless space, brought to his spirit a sense of rest and

peace.   The night was so serene, so calm, so passion-
less !   Everywhere the dominant moon silvered the
landscape with the distinctness of day.   The slopes
of the San Marcus hills stood revealed in the moonlight, and seemed to have encroached upon the level
plain, rimming the horizon with deepest blue.   The
live-oaks, dotting the prairie, stood out clearly, and
the mesquites appeared like shivering ghosts slipping
past him in the shadow.   It was very still.   The
thousand fragrant odors of the prairie rose upon him
as he rode forward.   Occasionally, the low hoot of an
owl, or the prolonged howl of a coyote, broke the
monotony.   He came suddenly upon a troop of mustangs, visiting a neighboring "salt-lick," and in an
instant the lonely waste awoke to life and animation.
The surprised *caballada* wheeled in the moonlight and
broke away with many a frisk and gambol.   From a
a spirit of emulation, Bruce put "Buckshot" to
his paces, and rode after them at the top of his
speed.

After a long, exhilarating canter, he checked his
panting horse and rode back upon his tracks.   The
excitement of the recent chase and the stimulus of
physical exercise had quite dispelled the feeling of
irritation which had driven him out of town at this
unseemly hour upon horseback.   Aside from his encounter in the sheriff's behalf, which had naturally
reacted somewhat upon his nerves, there were other
things which had tended to disturb the equanimity
of his temper.

As he rode on in the stillness, unbroken save by
the monotonous footfall of his horse, his thoughts
constantly reverted to Cynthia and her behavior with

the captain. It had annoyed him undeniably, and without his knowing why.

Bruce did not believe himself to be interested in Miss Dallas. Having little of that vanity which characterizes most men, it had probably never occurred to him, that much of Cynthia's apparent interest in Foraker was prompted by pique at his own refusal to act as her escort. He was aware that the quaint, breezy little maiden, who had rescued him so pluckily from his predicament in the Colorado, some months before, interested him greatly ; that he felt strangely drawn toward her, whenever he found himself in her society ; and that, being impelled by a thoroughly masculine impulse to favor her with sound advice and beneficial counsel, he was annoyed to find that she ignored it.

An incident of the early evening had not tended to increase the serenity of his temper. It was when, upon first recognizing Cynthia at the ball in company with Foraker, he had so far forgotten himself in his suspicion of the man as to inquire :

" Who is that fellow, Cynthia ? "

" A gentleman," Miss Dallas replied, provokingly. The rebuke was crushing. He writhed under it now at the recollection.

But, doubtless, what most annoyed Bruce was Cynthia's appearing in public with the man against whom he had taken the trouble to warn her. On behalf of my sex, I may be pardoned the reflection that the perversity of woman is often vexatious, and that the cheerful obstinacy with which they ignore common sense quite frequently paralyzes masculine prudence.

The sudden hoof-beats of a horse caused him to look up. So absorbed had he been in his reflections that he had taken no heed of his surroundings. He found himself on the San Marcus highway, at some distance from the town. A horseman was coming toward him, mounted upon a powerful gray. The moonlight glanced upon the epaulets and other decorations of the rider. The cause of his evening's annoyance stood before his eyes.

Captain Jack Foraker was evidently the worse for his evening's gayety. He had spent the latter portion of the night in visiting the neighboring saloons, and in monotonous patronage of the San Marcus bars. At length, being suddenly impressed with the necessity of presenting himself for roll-call at the garrison, he had reeled to the stable, kicked the sleepy ostler into consciousness, and rolling his semi-inebriated person into the saddle, started out of town an hour before sunrise.

It was this exhilarated individual, with difficulty bestriding his gallant gray charger, who encountered Henry Bruce a half-hour later on the San Marcus road. It was this gentleman who, instantly recognizing him in the clear light of the moon, drew rein to intercept him; and it was he who accosted him angrily, albeit incoherently, having apparently some grievance for which he wished redress.

Bruce, at once noting the condition of the redoubtable captain, turned his horse aside and endeavored to pass him without replying; but Foraker, perceiving his intent, put spurs to his gray and cannoned into him with a force that compelled him to halt.

"What do you mean by that?" demanded Bruce,

with difficulty reining in the prancing "Buckshot" after the collision.

"I've got suthin' to say to you, young feller," said the captain, thickly, rising in his stirrups, and leaning forward over the neck of his horse in an aggressive way. He emphasized his remarks with his heavy riding-whip. "You insulted me to-night. I want you to und'shtan' I'm a West-Point'r, and a damned sight too good company for any girl, you or any other tender-foot eshcorts to a ball. You hear me?" he demanded, with drunken directness, raising his voice. "Wass more, she ain't much on looks anyway, nor style either; and there wasn't any occasion for you to be so damned e'sclusive." Then, leaning over his saddle with an insulting air of giving very important advice, "You want to be devilish careful, young feller, or you'll get yourself into trouble—mind *that*."

"Stand aside!" Bruce broke in sternly, reining back his horse as if about to ride on.

"Tryin' to get away!" said the captain, with a sneer, attempting to intercept him by keeping his gray in front of him with whip and spur—"tryin' to get away—are ye? I want you to und'shtan', young feller, you can't do that until I'm done with you. I want you to und'shtan'—"

But here Bruce struck "Buckshot" sharply and attempted to dash by him.

The captain saw his intent, and, striking his spurs into his horse, made an effort to stop him a second time, by running into him. The effort proved futile. "Buckshot" had already got under way. Enraged at his want of success, Foraker rose in his stirrups, and, as Bruce passed him, struck him over the head with his heavy riding-whip, summoning to the effort all the strength he could muster.

The blow made Bruce reel in his saddle. For a moment he feared he should be unseated. The next, wheeling his horse about, he dashed against Foraker, closing with him in a mounted struggle for the whip.

As the horses came together, Bruce saw the captain shift his whip to his left hand suddenly, and caught the ominous glitter of a revolver in the light of the moon. He had barely time to crouch in the saddle when the weapon was fired, the bullet whistling close above his head. Clearly, the time for temporizing had passed. Forbearance was now suicidal. In an instant Bruce had drawn his own pistol, and, as the captain raised his arm a second time, he leveled it upon him.

The two weapons exploded simultaneously—the flash from his opponent's revolver almost blinding Bruce as the deafening reports rang out upon the still air. At the sound of the shots the horses sprang apart, and, through the smoke that hung heavily between them, Bruce could see the captain endeavoring with difficulty to keep the saddle. Hardly had he realized that he was himself unhurt, when Foraker swayed suddenly in his stirrups and fell heavily to the ground. The gray trotted off a few paces, and then stopped quietly to graze.

Bruce threw himself from his horse and bent over the prostrate man. The captain was lying upon his face, his hand still grasping the revolver. A slight smoke issued from the damp barrel. As he turned the body over, something warm fell upon his hand,

causing him an indescribable thrill. It was blood—
from a wound in the breast. The red drops were
trickling fast over the front of his uniform. Foraker
was dead.

Notwithstanding the justice of his action, Bruce
rose to his feet with an overmastering feeling of awe.
As he stood gazing down at the dead man, and the
eyes, so lately opened upon him in hate, stared blankly up into his, he tottered and felt faint. White as
was the face of the dead, his own was yet whiter, and
took on a ghastly expression in the cold, gray light
that seemed suddenly to possess earth and sky. Bruce
gazed vacantly about him and realized that it was
morning. A faint flush was visible in the east.

It was no sense of guilt, but the sickening realiza-
tion of having sent a human being to his long account,
that made his heart heavy as he mounted again and
rode slowly back along the level road; it was the
horror of the thing. So far as the act itself was concerned, it was clearly justifiable. It had been done
in self-defense.

His mind was made up as to what he should do.
He would ride back to San Marcus, seek out Sheriff
Mosely, acknowledge the shooting and the circumstances, and give himself up. For a moment his
courage misgave him, as he realized that there had
been no witness to the encounter, and that his justifi-
cation must rest upon his own unsupported statement.
He was pondering this fact with deep and increasing
misgiving, as he rode forward, when a familiar voice
hailed him just ahead, so abruptly as to startle him
and cause him to stop short. Four mounted men
had halted on the highway in front of him. It was

now broad daylight. Bruce recognized the familiar figure of Ike Mosely in the man who had addressed him. His deputies, Jake Sharp and "Humly Jim," were assisting him as mounted escort, in conducting the horse-thief, Lem Wickson, to the military jail at Bradford Post.

"How now, pardner?" remarked Mr. Mosely, genially, slipping one foot free from the leather stirrup, and throwing his leg easily over the pommel of his saddle; "yer takin' rather an early constitutional, ain't ye, fur one who's been up pretty near all night? I ain't specially fond of ridin' before breakfast myself, but Lem, here, was so anxious about gettin' into comfortable quarters, I reckoned we'd better humor him, so we've started for the Post. P'raps you'll reconsider on thet position of yours last night, and be willin' to celebrate thet pistol trick with a leetle genooine opedeldock."

He produced the well-known flask as he spoke, and extended it hospitably toward him.

Bruce could hardly force a smile at the sheriff's facetiousness. However, he took the flask and drank a swallow of its contents. It braced his nerves. In a few words he recounted what had happened.

"Ye don't say!" remarked Mosely, when he had finished. "So ye called Foraker in, eh?—jest natch-'ally dropped him, right in his tracks, when he had a bead on you fust? Wal, now, pardner, I congratulate you. Ef you'd like a recommend to jine 'the Rangers,' any time you're up our way, I reckon Ike Mosely will be on hand with the necessary papers.—I tell you what, boys," he said, turning round in the saddle suddenly, and addressing the two deputies,

"thet's rather sarcastic on a West-Pointer, rakin' a
soger out of his boots, when he was fust with his
weapon !"

Jake Sharp and "Humly Jim," seeing that the
great man was disposed to be jovial, received the reflection with ghastly merriment.

"How's thet ?" ejaculated Mosely, turning again
to Bruce, as the latter repeated his intention of giving
himself up. "You're thinkin' of comin' along with
us ? I reckon we've got about all we kin take care of
to-day;" winking craftily at the deputies. "Lem,
here, 's a big contract to handle, and it's pretty good
and free country all round about here. My eyes
sorter failin' me after last night's business, and my
hearin' bein' onsartin, I don't know ez I hev any
knowledge of this onexpected meetin' out here on the
road. I reckon, *ef I should ever get to hear* of any
sech encounter, it might be necessary fur me to take
some action ; but ez the case stands jest now, ye see,
I'm not aware thet anything out of the ornery hez occurred."

In spite of the sheriff's humorous reception of the
event of the early morning, Bruce still persisted in
his plan of giving himself up, urging that this was
the best and most honorable way of clearing himself
from the imputation of foul play. To this the genial
Ike cheerfully opposed the folly of any one's putting
himself in the clutches of the law for killing his adversary in a fair fight, and the risk of exposing himself to the infuriated soldiery at the Post, who would
naturally feel a partisan resentment at the death of
their chief.

Finding at length that Bruce was determined,

Mosely reluctantly acquiesced, but insisted that he should accompany them as if merely a traveling companion and not under arrest. Bruce was about to comply, when it suddenly dawned upon him that he was riding "Buckshot," and that he might be suspected of having stolen the horse—an act generally regarded by Lone Star tribunals to be less justifiable than actual homicide. He explained his position to the sheriff.

"Don't let thet worry you," replied that worthy, quickly, cutting the Gordian knot of the difficulty with official promptitude. "Ef you're bound to make me arrest ye, thet matter's easily settled. Freeze to the critter, pardner, for the rest of this trip. The State allows me to provide the means of bringin' in my prisoners, understand? It won't bother Jerrold much. I reckon I'll attach the animal fur your partickler benefit."

XII

THE event of the San Marcus ball had not proved entirely satisfactory to Cynthia, nor her stay with Miss Bertha Maverick an unalloyed delight. She returned to the Dallas Ranch with a very decided feeling of disappointment. Perhaps the behavior of Alcides on the evening in question sensibly aggravated this state of mind.

The door had hardly closed on the departing Foraker, when the old man presented himself, gun in hand, before the astonished Maverick household, and excitedly announced his intention of taking his daughter back home with him that very night. In vain Cynthia pleaded fatigue, and Miss Bertha declared that the festivities of the week were not ended; in vain the accommodating blacksmith extended to Alcides the hospitalities of his dwelling, and urged that it was too late altogether to think of attempting the journey; the old man remained obdurate, and there was nothing to do but comply.

It will be understood, by my feminine readers, that the young lady did this with a very ill grace, and that she rose rather late upon the following day, a little fretful and cross in consequence.

"I suppose them ear-rings didn't fetch thet Foraker to the extent she expected," commented Alcides, who was making preparations to ride into town for some family stores he had forgotten. The elder Dallas referred to some jewelry of glaring pattern he had recently purchased for Cynthia. He was not altogether confident of the purity or appropriateness of his own taste. He continued his preparations for departure, but was quietly observant and critical.

Miss Dallas took no notice of the solicitude of her sire. She was annoyed and displeased for many reasons : at her father, for his abrupt termination of her visit ; at Henry Bruce, for not proffering the attentions she had determined beforehand to thwart ; at the captain, for his susceptibility to the attractions of other belles, and his disposition to be convivial while in her company. Cynthia was too experienced in the society of the frontier to be either puritanical or prudish in the matter of beverages, but she resented the captain's indulgence, under the circumstances, with the sincerity it deserved.

Then there were other matters of solicitude—not so apparent to the masculine mind, but which a sympathetic sex will readily appreciate—matters between herself and Miss Bertha, wherein the rival charms of the young ladies had come in collision, resulting in consequent jealousy and woe.

The agony of mind, induced by such a succession of causes, is readily apparent ; so that later, when Mr. Buck Jerrold suddenly rode up to the ranch-gate and threw himself from the saddle, he was welcomed with a cordiality that might have been misleading.

"What hoss ye got thar, Buck ?" inquired Alcides, suspiciously, noting the enthusiasm of his daughter's manner. "Ain't thet Foraker's gray ?"

"I reckon *so*," Mr. Jerrold returned, with a gravity of manner that impressed both Alcides and Cynthia—"I reckon *so*, Al, and I don't wonder ye ask me. The fact is, so much hez taken place sence last night, thet I kin hardly git it straight myself or git started to tell it. I'm ridin' thet hoss because I've got permission from Jedge Pemberton to do so, and because Ike Mosely hez seized 'Buckshot' to transport a prisoner to the jail at Bradford Post."

He glanced quickly at Cynthia.

" To cut a long story short," he continued, averting his eyes from the girl's face, " Jack Foraker was found lyin' dead on the prairie, this mornin', with a bullet-wound in his left breast. His hoss was grazin' quietly in the neighborhood. Thar wasn't any explanation of the shootin', and all sorts of theories were flyin' about at San Marcus, when a couple of fellers rode into town and allowed, thet they met Ike Mosely and his deputies half-way to the Post, and thet they hed the man who done it."

" And who was it ? " asked Alcides, breathlessly.

Buck Jerrold glanced again at Cynthia. She was seated on the door-stone of the ranch, with clasped hands and startled eyes, noting every detail of the intelligence.

"I don't know nothin' about the matter myself, one way or t'other," responded Buck, turning his eyes inward as if to escape the imputation of being responsible for what he was about to communicate, "but Ridge Bartram said thet the man they hed was ridin' 'Buckshot,' and thet he hed confessed to hevin' shot Foraker in a hand-to-hand fight on hossback early this mornin'."

"*But who was it?*" Cynthia broke in impatiently.

"Henry Bruce," said Jerrold, quietly.

There was a dead silence. Dallas and Jerrold exchanged glances. A moment later Cynthia rose to her feet, white as the neighboring wall, and ran quickly into the house. In the hush that followed her departure the two men grew restless.

The old man was the first to speak, and when he did so, it was in tones of exultation.

"Wal, dern my skin, ef thet young feller don't deserve the thanks of the entire county!" he exclaimed, slapping his leg in self-congratulation over Foraker's untimely decease. "I allers *did* take consider'ble stock in Henry Bruce, and now I'm a tenderfoot, ef he ain't riz in my estimation a clean hundred per cent!"

Buck Jerrold assented with less emphasis. He was pondering the absence of Cynthia.

"Thar's no discountin' the fact thet Jack Foraker's death's a public benefit," he replied, with cheerful philosophy. "But I reckon, Al, thar's a good many ez is takin' pretty hard the mess young Bruce hez got himself inter. It seemed to break the Kernochans up pretty bad, and Miss Stafford was plumb beside herself. They left town fur the 'Mesquite Ranch,' ez soon ez they learned the facts; and Phil Kernochan said he was goin' to the Post arterwards."

A slight rustling in the direction of Cynthia's bedroom showed that Mr. Jerrold's facts were noted.

"Dog gone it, Buck, ye're right!" exclaimed Alcides, suddenly, as the possible danger of Bruce's position suggested itself to his mind. "Them sogers of

12

Foraker's company might take it into their cussed
heads to be ugly, and then thar's no tellin' what they
mightn't jest natch'ally do."

He turned his dull eyes toward the river, and devoted some moments to profound meditation.

"I'm not so sure it wouldn't be a right smart idea
to let Colonel Hunt and his rangers know how matters stand," he suggested. He glanced inquiringly at
Jerrold. That gentleman appeared lost in thought.
"Wal, I reckon I'll go to town and see what's the
latest developments," he said, finally. "Hedn't ye
better go 'long?"

Mr. Jerrold reflected. He would have much preferred a half-hour's conversation with Cynthia, but
the occasion was evidently not a propitious one. Since
the delivery of his unwelcome intelligence, he had seen
nothing of her. He lounged idly about the door a
few minutes, in the hope that she might come out.
She did not appear. So he turned reluctantly to accompany Alcides.

The old man had already mounted the box-seat of
his wagon, and taken up the reins. He whipped up
smartly, and, with a loud protest from axle and spring,
the crazy conveyance got fairly under way. Jerrold
tarried only to cast one regretful glance in the direction of Cynthia's window; then, mounting the gray,
he dashed after him down the road. In a few minutes the figures of both men were lost to view in the
shrubbery that bordered the river.

The house grew strangely quiet after their departure. The ebony Amelia had departed early that morning for a day's holiday at San Marcus, so the busy
sounds of the kitchen were hushed. The hens and

chickens, taking advantage of her absence, strolled boldly about the door-yard, and camped out and foraged among the pots and pans, after the fashion of neglected poultry. The antelope tugged at his confining tether, missing the attentions of his mistress. "Aulus" dozed, and caught flies on the door-step. A general air of reposeful indifference seemed to have settled down upon the Dallas ranch with the sunbeams that slumbered on its porch.

It was late in the afternoon when the door opened suddenly, and Cynthia came out. She was dressed as for a journey. She wore the long habit familiar to her riding excursions, and, as she stepped from the door-stone, her daintily gathered skirts revealed diminutive riding-boots and silver spurs. Beyond a slight redness of the eyelids, there was no trace of the agitation of a few hours before, but, in place of it, a settled resolve shone in her eyes, and spoke in her movements. She passed quickly across the door-yard, heedless of the gambols of "Aulus" and the bleats of the tethered antelope. Arriving at the barn in the rear of the ranch, she roused herself sufficiently to shut the great hound in a neighboring box-stall, and hook the door securely ; whereupon, without further delay, she led her pony from the stable, and saddled and bridled him as fast as her eager fingers could manipulate buckle and strap. She accomplished this task with a deft ease to which habit had long accustomed her. With equal readiness she led the obedient mustang to an adjacent tree-stump, where she effected successfully the somewhat discommoding achievement of mounting. Then, with a sharp cut of her riding-whip, she started "Pepita" at once into a gallop, and

struck out over the prairie with a directness that
showed her fixedness of purpose.

Her mind was made up; she had decided what to
do. In the interval since she had learned of the misfortune that had overtaken Henry Bruce, she had
weighed the possible dangers of his position, and resolved that assistance must be sent him at all hazards.
The forebodings of Alcides were scarcely spoken when
they awoke the courage and sympathy of her resolute
little heart. She had waited only to see if her father
or Jerrold would return to send the warning the former had suggested. They had not done so. Roused
now to a fever of excitement at the delay, she had determined to be the bearer of the tidings herself.

To see Colonel Hunt, who was a friend of her
father's, and well known to Cynthia; to acquaint him
with the circumstances of the tragedy of the early
morning; to champion Bruce's cause to the utmost,
and so work upon the sympathies of the ranger captain that he would summon his men and go at once
to Bradford Post—this was the errand the courageous
girl had undertaken.

And now, as she set out upon this mad ride over
valley and divide, her pulses throbbed with anxiety
and her heart grew faint, fearing some possible mis-
chance that might cause the failure of her plan. What,
if the colonel should be absent ! What, if the rangers
had moved their camp from the locality she so well
knew, and had so often visited with her father ! What,
if some other warning had called these adventurous
men away from their headquarters, and she should
arrive to find the place a solitude, and herself power-
less to aid or to save him ! In terror at the thought,

she plied without pity both bit and spur. The panting "Pepita" fairly flew! Used as she was to the
saddle, the breathless haste, the agony of that terrible
gallop remained always an event in Cynthia's memory.
She heeded not the familiar landscape, undulating
ever before her like a billowy sea ; the alarmed cattle
that fled in a panic from the thunder of her approach ;
the occasional bands of antelope that dashed away,
affrighted ; the flocks of quail and summer duck that
whirred to the right and left, as she dashed through
copse and underbrush, or came suddenly upon some
outlying pool. On, on she sped, while the trees flew
reeling by, and the ravens croaked an ominous presage
from the wayside. "Pepita" was flagging a little.
She had still some miles to go. The sun was sinking
slowly but surely to the horizon. Yet, taking ever
with the skill of the frontier, the shortest and most
direct way to her rendezvous, plunging through chaparral at the peril of life and limb, her garments torn,
her pony bleeding from the thorny thicket, she still
held her course to the westward, and galloped on with
a courage that in man would have been heroic, but in
woman was sublime !

The camp, occupied by Colonel Hunt and the
rangers he commanded, was pitched in a motte of
pecans that bordered a fertile valley. The lofty tree-
tops lifted themselves—a dark-green barrier against
the monotony of the level plain. Within, the white
tents of the rangers glimmered in the shade, saddles
and camp-utensils were scattered about, horses stood
tethered here and there, or roamed with hoppled
limbs and tinkling stock-bell through the grove —

everything wore the air of a picturesque and favorable encampment.

It was the supper-hour, and camp-fires were beginning to illuminate the shadows of the aisles. The glancing light flashed upon the figures of the men, busied in cooking, or lounging in groups about the doors of their tents ; upon arms and accoutrements, stacked and piled against various trees. The fires roared and crackled ; the steam of the broiling morsels filled the air ; and in the background, where a somewhat larger and more comfortable tent stood by the side of a quiet pool, the rising globe of the silver moon swung silently over the forest picture.

The waters were already beginning to shimmer and dance with its reflected rays, when the flap of this tent was pushed aside, and a man strode out of the opening. As he did so the light of a camp-fire opposite flashed full upon him, and revealed the features of Colonel William Hunt.

It was a characteristic face. One understood, at a glance, why it was that this man had been chosen to lead the disciplined band that followed him. The locks that he bared to the evening air were a trifle grizzled with age. Hardship and privation had set their seal upon the face, but only to intensify its look of determination and daring. Decision and will dominated the strong lines of mouth and jaw. It was apparent at once that, whatever courage could undertake or energy achieve, yielded before the marked personality of the man.

Something of this was apparent in the glances cast upon him by his men, as he strode in among them and sauntered away through the trees. Their manner betokened a respect that the intimacy and familiarity of their camp-life could not dispel.

Colonel Hunt did not stop until he reached a large tree that stood like a giant picket upon the very confines of the grove. He leaned his back against it and stood looking out upon the shadowy plain which the moonlight was beginning to illumine. Hardly had he done so, when the rhythmic hoof-beats of a horse, coming toward him at full gallop, struck his ear. He stood erect and listened. A breeze had sprung up, and, as its light breath fanned his furrowed cheek, he could even distinguish the panting breath of the animal, as if driven hard or furiously ridden. Surprised that any one should be approaching the camp at such a rate of speed, he stepped out into the open. In an instant he was almost run down by Cynthia, mounted upon the foam-covered " Pepita."

The apparition of her mounted presence came upon Hunt so suddenly, that he cried out, " Halt ! " with the sternness of one used to command. The horse was checked instantly, but with a recklessness that almost threw the exhausted animal upon its haunches.

" Who's there ? " demanded the colonel, striding up.

For a few moments there was no reply. Then a voice in the gloom panted, " Cynthia ! " and immediately after, the girl slipped lightly to the ground, and stood leaning exhaustedly against the saddle.

She was so breathless and spent with the fatigue of her long ride that, at first, she could only indicate the urgency of her errand by broken sentences. Meanwhile the colonel, roused by the eloquence of her pale face and disheveled tresses, was moved to

sympathy. When, at last, with many pauses for
breath, but with an earnestness that betrayed her
anxiety, she had made her purpose known, the ranger's response was kindly and reassuring.

"Ye're a brave little girl," he said, "and a man
oughter feel proud that one o' your style takes the
trouble to show an interest in him. Well, Miss Cynthia, come up to the camp and we'll see what can be
done. It's a full moon to-night, and only a few
hours' hard riding from here to the Post. Perhaps
it'd be jest as well if I took the boys over for a little
pasear. They won't mind it much, and, even if nothing comes of it, it will set your fears at rest at any
rate. Ef thar's a man in my company that isn't willin' to make this trip, when he hears of the ride
you've taken to save Henry Bruce, he's not fit to serve
under Colonel Hunt, I'll be bound! You've struck
us at the right time, too, young lady. Supper is
waiting — such as it is! As soon as that is over,
we'll saddle up and start. Ez for yourself, I can send
you back by the night-coach thet passes Thompson's
Ranch about an hour from now, I reckon."

But here he paused, at a gesture of dissent from
Cynthia, who had taken the bridle of "Pepita" and
was already leading her into the grove.

"Send me back by the night-coach!" she repeated, glancing at him and knitting her brows.
"Thank you, sir, I'm not to be disposed of so easily.
I have friends at the Post, and reckon they'll be willing to take care of me to-night. At any rate, I'll
ask 'em. If you can give me a fresh horse, and it's
all the same to you, Colonel Hunt, I reckon I'll ride
along, too."

The tall ranger captain looked down at the resolution of the pale face lifted to his in the moonlight. The admiration that he felt for this Amazonian utterance shone in his face and glistened in his eyes. But the colonel's speech, like that of many decisive natures, was homely, and the tenor of his thought was not borne out by his words. He stared blankly at the surrounding trees, as if for confirmation of his own surprise. Apparently having received the assurance he desired, he shook his head and remarked, emphatically, " *Well, I'll be blowed !* "

With this characteristic utterance he quietly re-entered the grove.

XIII

THE full moon in meridian splendor shone calmly down at Bradford Post. The little plateau on which the frontier fort was placed stood out above the outlying country with all the distinctness of day. Seen from that elevated point, the waters of the Big and Little Fury glittered to their confluence at the base of the height ; the bridge at the crossing shone black among the trees ; and even the distant roofs of the town of Joaquin were clearly visible. The moonlight flooded everything within the Post itself, steeping the three sides of the level square, illuminating the low barracks of the soldiers and the adobe dwellings of the officers opposite, and slipping ghost-like from the white flag-staff, which seemed to stretch a spectral finger to the stars. It wanted yet two hours of midnight, but the lights were out which, earlier in the evening, had flickered in the various quarters. So gracious was the night, it seemed to breathe a benison upon the slumbers of the quiet garrison.

Yet there was commotion at Bradford Post—not within the confines of the fort itself, nor in the moonlit spaces of the level square, but far in the rear of the soldiers' barracks, where a small, low stone building stood with barred door and grated windows. A

crowd of fifty or sixty men were collected about this
structure, conversing in low tones and excitedly running from window to window. As they moved to
and fro, the rays of the moon flashed upon muskets
and accoutrements. They were the soldiers of Foraker's company, ripe for insurrection over the death
of their chief; and the building about which they
were gathered was the military jail of Bradford
Post.

Trouble had been brewing since early morning.
With the arrival of Sheriff Mosely and his prisoners,
the news of the tragedy at San Marcus had spread
like wild-fire through the camp. Foraker's men received the intelligence sullenly, but with evident suspicion of foul play. The dead captain had been popular with his company, which included the most reckless and desperate of the soldiers at the fort. There
were among them certain dissipated spirits who cherished a lively admiration for the hardihood and noto-
rious reputation of their leader. Considerable curiosity had been expressed in regard to the man who
had seen fit to abbreviate so enviable a career. There
had been trips to the jail in consequence, and throughout the day a crowd of eager faces had beset the windows. In consequence of the absence of the presiding justice, the time for a hearing in the case had been
set down for the following day. In the present state
of popular feeling, Sheriff Mosely had thought best to
confine the body of Bruce during the interval. He
had been obliged, therefore, to incarcerate him in the
single room of the jail in company with Lemuel Wickson. Through the heavily barred windows the forms
of the men could be dimly seen and even conversa-

tion interchanged through an occasional broken pane.

The soldiers had been in doubt, at first, as to which of the two was responsible for the death of the captain. Some vigorous personal criticism and animated invective, delivered through the windows, elicited the information required. Bruce had kept his own counsel, while Mr. Lemuel Wickson had replied cheerfully to this genial badinage. Being free to move about, he gratified his resentment against Bruce for his capture, by going to the window and giving whispered and startling accounts of the killing of Foraker. It appeared from these vivid word-pictures that the ex-horse-thief had been an eye-witness to the tragedy. His imagination was entirely responsible for his facts. Yet so cleverly did he work upon the excited sympathies of the indignant company, that by nightfall it was generally believed that Foraker had been butchered in cold blood while drunk and asleep. It was doubtful whether during the interval Mr. Wickson, by the invention of local color and realistic detail, had not persuaded himself of the truth of his statements. Sheriff Mosely and one deputy mounted guard during the day, and interposed a spirited but ineffectual denial to this version of the affair. Some local disturbance in the town of Joaquin had unfortunately necessitated the absence of Jake Sharp.

As the afternoon wore away, the feeling of animosity against Bruce grew more expressive and violent. The crowd of loungers about the jail increased. Personal abuse of the prisoner was indulged in at the windows, and even threats of violence were openly heard. Some of the boldest went so far as to counsel

Wickson to kill Bruce, declaring, with a mob's ready acceptance of responsibility, that they would "stand by him."

Mr. Wickson had expressed, in words, a cordial willingness to comply with these requests, but when it came to deeds, had shown a singular reluctance. He alleged as the reason for this delay the fact that he had no weapon ; but, as Bruce himself was unarmed, this statement was hardly pertinent. How far he was influenced by a certain cold glitter in the latter's eye did not transpire. The fact remains that he listened quietly to the urgent but impracticable advice of the soldiers to "cut the tenderfoot's heart out," to "throw the stove on him," and other unconsidered suggestions that were rained upon him all the afternoon. But at nightfall Mr. Wickson was still conspicuously doing nothing.

Then came a lull ; the men dispersed for supper. Sheriff Mosely availed himself of the interval to send a message of the state of things to the colonel at the fort, a message which that worthy unaccountably saw fit to disregard.

After this he loaded his extra pistols, and withdrew with "Humly Jim" to the little guard-room behind the outer door. Here he had recourse to his pocket-flask and philosophically awaited developments.

"I allow," he said, quietly, to his only remaining deputy, after participating with him in this refreshment, "thet we don't get through this night's bizness, natch'ally, without suthin' of a row ; but whatever happens, Jim, Ike Mosely don't reckon on bein' either euchred or bluffed. I don't propose to let Lem, thar, git out, and they can't have Henry Bruce except over my dead body. *Savey thet?*"

The deputy did.

"Now, what I expect of you, Jim," continued Ike, "is what I allers get—*cl'ar grit and nothin' else.*"

He leaned forward and gripped his ill-favored comrade's hand as he said this. The two men exchanged glances.

"Ef they start to break in here to-night, I'll draw them fastenings," pointing to the iron door that led into the room where the prisoners were confined, "and call on Henry Bruce. We two 'll keep this place against all comers or die together, you can take my word for thet! Your bizness 'll be to go in thar and hold thet tarrier, Wickson, and prevent his gittin' out. Ef he makes a break or acts anyway obstrep'rous, shoot him jest the same ez ye would a jack-rabbit. Thar ain't no other way with sich cattle. He's more'n half responsible for the trouble we're goin' to git to-night, and I only wish my 'six-shooter' hed sorter gone off by accident on the way up here. It would have saved my conscience consider'ble wear and tear. Ez it is now, I'm about cat up with remorse."

As the shadows of evening drew around the jail, the sheriff's forebodings seemed at first without foundation. With the beating of "taps," lights vanished at the fort, the sounds of frontier discipline were hushed, and the camp apparently sank to repose. Deceived by this absence of hostilities, the solitary deputy dozed on a bench of the low corridor. Only Ike Mosely remained alert and vigilant.

The moonbeams, stealing through the barred grating of the roof, were falling almost vertically upon the stone pavement at his feet, when his quick ear caught the sound of voices. Drawing a narrow slide in the outer door, he peered through its semicircular guard. A crowd of men were collected in front of the jail. They were conversing together in low tones. In the light of the moon the sheriff recognized several of the most desperate of Foraker's men. One burly fellow held in his hand a coil of rope. Closing the slide cautiously, he roused his companion and examined his pistols. A second later, the jail-door vibrated with a blow struck upon it by some heavy object from without.

"Who's there?" demanded Mosely, at the slide.

"Come, come, Ike Mosely," replied a loud voice, which the sheriff instantly recognized as the sergeant of Foraker's men; "this ain't no game of bluff. We're here for bizness, and we want you to open up."

"P'raps you'll state your reasons for gittin' in, before I give ye the privilege," responded Mosely.

"Wal, yes, we don't mind, seein' we're comin' in, whether you're willin' or not," responded the voice. "We're goin' to hang that damned tenderfoot, you've got in there, to the highest tree in the Post. That's what we're going to do! So we tell you to open up!"

"Oh, ye are?" said Ike, tauntingly. "Mebbe you reckon that I'll set quietly by and see you do all *thet?* Now, I'm givin' it to you straight, what you kin expect ef you try on anything of the kind. Thar's two of us, here, and *we'll kill every mother's son of ye thet gets in, ez sure ez there's a living God!*"

A blow from the outside was the only response.

"Thet's right!" shouted Ike, as a second blow caused the door to spring on its hinges. "The sooner ye make a hole through thet partition, the more likely I am to reach ye!"

He emphasized the remark by drawing the slide and discharging his revolver through the aperture. A yell, and a sudden shuffling of feet without greeted the shot.

For a time all was quiet. Mosely drew the slide again, and reconnoitred. The result was apparently not satisfactory. He snapped the catch back suddenly, and turned sharply upon "Humly Jim."

"It's jest ez I reckoned," he said, quietly; "they're comin' back agin, and, this time, they've got a timber with 'em, and thet door is goin' in. I reckon it's high time for us to make a division of forces."

He drew the bolts on the inner door, as he spoke.

"Call him," he whispered.

"Humly Jim" complied. A second later Bruce stepped through the opening. The deputy grasped his revolvers, and disappeared within. Ike Mosely turned and faced the ranchman in the moonlight.

"Pardner," he said, placing his hands upon his shoulders, and gazing into his eyes, "ye don't need me to tell ye, thet this'll be a close call for you and me, and mebbe one or both of us is goin' home. But, by the living God! I'm here to tell ye, thet thar's no man I'd rather fight for, or die alongside!"

He pressed a pair of "six-shooters" into his companion's hands, as he spoke.

"Now then," he said, setting his square shoulder against the shoulder of Bruce, and cocking his pistols, "let 'em come on, damn 'em! They'll find they've got more than they bargained for, or else I've forgotten how to shoot!"

A rush from without drowned his words, as a blow, delivered with the force of a battering-ram, caused the door to leap inward. A shower of dust and plastering fell to the floor. A second rush and shock followed. The door fell from its hinges with a crash, and the moon shone boldly in and streamed upon the stone pavement. Bruce and Mosely retreated into the shadows of the doorway. Here, unseen by those without, they covered the entrance with their cocked revolvers. The moonlight flashed coldly on the glistening barrels, full in the sight of an excited crowd of men poising a heavy beam.

A moment's pause ensued. The soldiers, thinking that the weapons were those of the sheriff and his deputy, and that Bruce was in the interior of the jail, were averse to unnecessary bloodshed. At this instant there was a crash of musketry in the rear, accompanied by the jingling of glass and the whistling of bullets. The leader of the party held up his hand to parley.

"I reckon you hear that, Ike Mosely," he said, with an oath. "The boys are rakin' your lock-up from the windows. You might ez well hand that feller over quiet and peaceable, before they take him out a corpse. We've sworn to string him up, and, ez we're ten to your one, ye might as well be sensible and give in."

"You think so, do you?" retorted the sheriff, through his set teeth. "I'll let you know *I* think different! I'll allow thet me and Jim can't hold but one end of this jail, but thet's about what we calcu-

late to do. Of course, ef you kill him in the mean
time, I ain't responsible, but the first man of you thet
steps across thet door-sill is gone in—I give you thet
flat!"

The sheriff had hardly spoken, when the door of
the inner room swung quickly back, and "Humly
Jim" appeared. He was not visible to the throng
without. Closing the door behind him, he leaned
against it. His voice came distinctly to the ears of
Mosely and Bruce.

"Thar ain't no use for me to put in any more
time in thar," he said, slowly. "Thar ain't no prisoner to guard. Leastwise, none thet's likely to git
away. Thet last volley settled Lem's account for
good and all, I reckon. The durned idgits killed the
wrong man! P'raps, thet bein' the case, you've got
more use for me here in front."

Mosely was about to whisper some hurried command to his deputy, when a second volley crashed
through the inner room, splintering the wood-work
and beams. The sounds of this terrific fusillade had
not entirely ceased, before a sudden noise, borne on
the night wind, came to their ears from without. A
loud rumble, as of distant thunder, shook the earth,
and the windows of the jail rattled with a strong vi-
bratory tremor. The crowd about the shattered door
turned in surprise. A clear, ringing cheer burst suddenly upon the still night. There were the sound of
galloping hoofs and the murmur of many voices, and
with a sudden rush and tumult a mounted cavalcade
swept round the jail, the moonlight flashing upon
their brandished rifles. In an instant the building
was surrounded.

The leader of the party charged the group of soldiers before the doorway at a gallop, reining up his horse so fiercely that the hoofs of the animal struck fire in the resisting gravel.

"Fall back!" shouted the imperative voice of Colonel Hunt. "Clear out, now, all of you, and disperse! This business has gone far enough."

At the sharp command, Foraker's men, realizing they were now between two fires, scattered in all directions. The soldiers in the rear of the jail were as quickly routed. Hardly three minutes elapsed before the horseman threw himself from the saddle, and, striding over the fallen door, entered the corridor.

"Just in time, Ike, to put a stop to this yer foolishness," he remarked, grasping the sheriff by the hand.

"Not much too late, Bill, thet's a fact," replied Mosely, returning the greeting. "'Pon my word, colonel, I rather looked for somethin' of a scrimmage, but this sudden freak o' yours for a moonlight *pasear* sorter took the sand out o' them sojers, natch'ally, didn't it? What angel sent you down our way at this hour of the night?"

Colonel William Hunt removed his hat, and the moonlight shone full upon his serious face.

"You've struck it, Mosely!" he said, solemnly. "An out-and-out angel—and no mistake! I ain't no call to take to myself any credit for this yer night's business. It all belongs to a *woman*—a little gal ez galloped ten miles to bring me word, and, notwithstanding, hez rid with us every step of the way, and put the blush to every man in my troop—a gal ez I'd bank on ag'in half the men I ever see, and who's too good a durned sight for the best man in the State ! "

And, even at this moment, pale, breathless, and disheveled, Cynthia Dallas staggered trembling to the doorway, and sank fainting on the threshold.

XIV

WITH the arrival of the rangers and their armed investment of the jail at Bradford Post, the open animosity against Henry Bruce vanished. Such was the awe inspired by these frontier police, that no further attempt at outbreak followed. At nine o'clock of the following day, a mounted escort accompanied Bruce to the court-house, and a preliminary examination was held. Phil Kernochan had arrived during the night, bringing with him Judge Natchez, the ablest lawyer of the circuit. The prisoner found himself surrounded by influential counsel and friends.

The presiding justice conducted the proceedings with that perfect impartiality and absence of judicial dignity for which he was noted. With his hat on the back of his head, a short, black pipe in his mouth, and untrammeled by coat, cravat, or collar, he lent himself seriously to the gravity of the occasion. A proposal, on the part of the prosecuting attorney, to adjourn court until they had shared the hospitality of the neighboring saloon, was frowned upon severely by this Texan Rhadamanthus. The district attorney was a bosom friend of Foraker, and hostile to Bruce.

How far the judicial mind may have been influenced by this significant fact, by the sullen presence of the more disaffected of Foraker's men in the court-room, and by the armed demonstration of the night before, it is impossible to determine.   Judge Pemberton smoked, alike impassively, through the eloquent argument of the prisoner's counsel and the fiery appeal of the State's representative.   But, on motion of Judge Natchez to release Bruce on bail, he cheerfully acquiesced.   He further agreed to the application for a change of venue, holding that the present state of popular feeling was hardly conducive to that calmness of deliberation which the law prescribes.

His Honor's phraseology is necessarily lost in the above paraphrase.   He said, I believe, that he "wasn't tryin' no case, in no place, where everybody was dead sot on hangin' the prisoner first, and holdin' court arterwards."   But, doubtless, the legal principle of abstract justice was implied in this Lone Star dictum. The trial was set down for the first week in September, at the neighboring county-seat of Oskaloo.

Sheriff Mosely was overjoyed at this decision.

"Why, thet's right whar I was born and brought up," he said to Bruce, slapping him on the back as they left the court - room.   "I own thet place. Yer hand, pardner ; I congratulate you on yer luck. When the time comes round, I'll run down thar and see ef I can't scare up a reasonable, fa'r-minded, and onprejudiced jury, ez'll view this business in a true and holy light."

The confidence of Bruce in his eventual acquittal, united to his own conviction of the justice of his cause, was naturally increased by this reassuring statement.

None the less did Phil Kernochan relax his exertions in his partner's behalf. He consulted earnestly with Colonel Hunt, who, with a party of his men, conducted them back to the "Mesquite Valley Ranch." Judge Natchez—a man of wide experience in Texan practice and pleading—outlined several modes of action, but was inclined to lay considerable stress upon Sheriff Mosely's co-operation, and suggested that Mr. Buck Jerrold be approached as a possible valuable ally. Accordingly, a few days later, Kernochan rode over to the latter's ranch and held a conference with that gentleman.

Mr. Jerrold had been already importuned in behalf of Henry Bruce. He had paid a visit to the Dallas Ranch, the previous evening, and had heard from Cynthia's own lips an account of the storming of the jail at Bradford Post, and the rescue that followed. So pathetically had Cynthia wrought upon the sympathies of her auditor, that Jerrold had been unable to resist the appeal. It was, perhaps, proof positive of the cow-man's love for Miss Dallas and his own generosity of soul, that he promised his assistance, although in giving it he was aware that he stood in his own light.

He received Kernochan with that gravity of demeanor for which he was noted, tempered, possibly, with a certain resignation which, under the circumstances, increased the latter's good opinion. Kernochan unfolded his errand in a few words. Buck Jerrold filled his pipe, lighted it, and, seating himself on a nail-keg in the door-yard, reviewed the situation solemnly as follows :

"Thar ain't but one argyment to bring to bear on the town of Oskaloo," he said, deliberately, crossing his legs—" and thet's *whisky!* I've been down thar, off and on, for the last ten years, and I never knew anythin' else to carry conviction in thet thrivin' settlement—onless it was a 'six-shooter,' and even then, I reckon, whisky 'd stand the best show. Ye see," he said, pulling at the straps of his heavy boots, and glancing at them, as if for inspiration, " the poppylation is thet rigid and narrer-minded, that it needs suthin' of thet nature to get the milk o' human kindness to flow. They want suthin' to *start 'em!* I've seen 'free whisky in the back room,' at Oskaloo, do more for bizness on a cash basis, than low prices and onlimited credit. It's the same way with lawin'. I ain't no drinkin' man, Mr. Kernochan, ez you know ; I don't drink, because—because—" said Mr. Jerrold, reflectively, raising his eyes to Kernochan and deliberately closing one quietly—"*because I don't.* But I recognizes the value of licker in makin' an idee popular, and, so to speak, creatin' a majority. Ef I could go down thar, now, in the interests of justice, and jest float the town ; jest play the millionaire and do the generous thing—it might cost you suthin'—but I reckon—I reckon—" said Mr. Jerrold, cautiously— " we *might* get an honorable and squar deal, even in thet benighted settlement.

"It's ag'in the natur o' things," continued Mr. Jerrold, "to look for favorable results on any other ground. Them fellers down thet way, I reckon, are what Parson Centrefitt calls '*pestimists*'—they're malarial in their tastes, and they'd get things crooked on gen'ral principles. Accordin' to their view, everything is cross-grained from the start. They jest natch'ally look at things on the bias—so to speak.

They'd allow, for instance, thet Henry Bruce layed all night for Foraker, out on the San Marcus road ; thet he rounded him up, and started him on the 'long trail,' because he was stampedin' his plans and prospects. Thet's what *they'd* ha' done, and thet's the way they'd look at it. You and me knows different— thet it was done in self-defense. But it'll need judicious maniperlatin' to make 'em thet liberal-minded, and to git 'em at all charitably disposed. They must be elevated to thet p'int. *Then* ye'll git justice. Their moral natur sorter leaves off where the rest of us begin."

He paused, and looked seriously at Kernochan to note the effect of his words. Evidently gathering that, from his visitor's previous opinion of the town of Oskaloo, his logic was beginning to tell on him, he summed up his position in a few words :

"Ef I rec'lect, I was a leetle onsettled myself, thet night, in San Marcus, and I ain't no way sartin thet Henry Bruce didn't take a gratifyin' contract off my hands. You go to work, Mr. Kernochan, and engage the best lawyers and argifyers the State can produce. Them'll be necessary, ez the prosecuting attorney is dead ag'in ye from the fust. But, ez for the Oskaloo part of the bizness, me and Ike Mosely'll run thet. And I reckon," concluded Mr. Jerrold, rising and permitting a grim smile to relax the corners of his mouth—"*I reckon the jury at thet trial will be in compytent hands.*"

Phil Kernochan rode back to his ranch, under the impression that the difficulty of combating local prejudice at Oskaloo was materially lessening. But Mr. Buck Jerrold was gloomy and dispirited all the afternoon.

It was not long before the delight with which Miss
Stafford greeted the release of Henry Bruce gave place
to a very different state of mind.   In the enthusiasm
of his return to the "Mesquite Valley Ranch," she
had detected no change in his manner toward her.
Accustomed from infancy to her own way, the idea of a
rival, in the regard she unquestionably manifested for
the young ranchman, had, probably, never seriously
crossed her mind.   She had accepted the interest of
Bruce complacently, laid claim to his attentions, as if
by a species of divine right, and exhibited toward
him a certain air of proprietorship, with the presump-
tion of the sex when conscious of its attractions.   To
quote the words of Judge Natchez, who was, for professional reasons, some time a guest at the "Mesquite
Valley Ranch," the young lady's attitude toward
Henry Bruce was that of the "holder of a first-mort-
gage bond, wherein the equity was decidedly micro-
scopic."

Miss Stafford very soon awoke to an intelligent
distrust of her position, and then to a conviction that
her power was on the wane.   Her mortification and
chagrin, to find herself supplanted by one whom her
pride, in no sense, recognized as an equal, can well be
imagined.

Perhaps the first intimation that Edith received
of a change in Bruce was in his manner of receiving
her slighting allusions and half-contemptuous mention of Miss Dallas.   Originally, he had passed these
over with the good-humored cynicism of a man of
the world.   But, now, anything of the sort plainly
irritated him, and persistence in the matter provoked
a retort, or possibly a sudden sarcasm.   With singular

infelicity of epithet, Miss Stafford had characterized
Cynthia's devotion to Bruce, during his imprison-
ment, as "*kind*"—"really quite what one would
have expected a girl of her surroundings to have
done."

It will be understood that Bruce—having passed
his early life amid the same surroundings as Miss
Stafford, and not having found the modern society
belle particularly generous or self-sacrificing—cherished a different sentiment.

His old interest in Cynthia—the interest that he
had felt since that first day, when she had peeped
down upon him in the gloomy chasm, with her fragrant suggestions of hemlock and pine—woke anew
in his heart, and with it a sense of gratitude, from
which, I trust, mankind, in the rarity of feminine
constancy, is not entirely exempt. This interest deep-
ened as the spring advanced and the season slipped
into summer. He grew quite in the habit of riding
over to the Dallas Ranch and passing the morning
in Cynthia's society. Here, although he persuaded
himself that his attitude toward the young lady was
merely such as a brother might assume toward an
affectionate sister, he was often astounded to discover
with what winged feet the hours flew overhead, and
that familiar objects took on a sudden association and
charm from the witchery of her company.

It was, doubtless, this brotherly interest in Miss
Dallas that prompted Henry Bruce to instruct her
upon the guitar—an instrument singularly calculated
to overcome shyness and restraint between persons of
the opposite sex, and as such to be commended. If,
while thus employed, Cynthia found herself sitting,

at times, very near Bruce, and their fingers dangerously involved, in compelling melody from the refractory strings, it was unquestionably due to her
anxiety to become a proficient performer. And if,
while playing some chord or explaining some accom-
paniment, there stole into the gentleman's face an
expression, so winning and tender that the girl's
sweet eyes grew downcast and tremulous, it was the
zeal of the instructor, doubtless, that prompted this.
Certainly, for its opportunities and possibilities, the
light guitar has reason to be appreciated ; and there
slumbers in its strings a sympathy that proves a
powerful ally to sentiment.

Howbeit, whatever may have been the experience
of her companion, Cynthia learned little from the
instrument of which her heart had not been eloquent
before.   But she acquired a certain dainty dexterity,
and as this musical intercourse gave rise to much conversation and confidential disclosure, it was not long
before Bruce was well acquainted with all her girlish
dreams and fancies—except one, in regard to which
Cynthia said nothing, but preserved the evasive silence
of womankind.

It shone in her eyes that kindled at his coming ;
in the quick color that mounted to her cheek at his
approach ; in the sudden delicious tremor that seized
her when he drew near ; and the indescribable thrill
that set her heart to throbbing whenever his hand
touched hers.   In place of that dejection that once
oppressed her, a glad gayety and light-heartedness attended all her movements.   Joy laughed in the sunlight and mirth came to her on the wings of the wind.
The breeze that rocked the tree-tops of her bower,

letting slip bright shafts of light to stray within, set her all unconsciously to singing.

Old man Dallas noted the change, and grew reserved and thoughtful. After Cynthia's daring ride to Bradford Post, he had taken occasion to read his charming daughter a long homily on the "danger of young women showin' all to onct how much store they set by any young feller." According to Alcides, it was the duty of the sex to "set back and let things hump themselves according to their natch'ral course." Cynthia had accepted this rebuke meekly. She was now uniformly affectionate to her father.

"I reckon them new bonnets she was talkin' about must have got up to San Marcus," remarked this cautious skeptic, who was inclined to refer all feminine advances to mercenary motives. Finding, however, that his daughter's caresses were quite gratuitous, he shook his head gravely with renewed distrust. It was only after a doleful rehearsal upon his fiddle of his symphony to "Married Life," that he appeared to have pierced the heart of the mystery.

It was about this time that Miss Stafford ceased to allude to the frequency of the visits paid Miss Dallas by Henry Bruce ; it was about this time that she became apparently unaware that any such young woman existed ; it was about this time that she began to drop stray hints in regard to certain admirers at the North, for whom she cherished an extravagant interest—an interest which speedily began to manifest itself in correspondence ; it was about this time that she gave out that these parties were importuning her greatly to return home ; but before doing so, she meditated a *coup d'état* by which she trusted to wring the heart of her rival, and, if possible, "lure this tassel gentle back again."

Meanwhile, all unconsciously the summer waxed and waned. Days of endless blue and staring sunlight dropped the green mantle from the hills, replacing it with the tawny robe the sirocco lends. At times the cool night-breezes brought with them a train of mists that held a ghostly dance beneath the moon, but fled dismayed at early morning and trooped forlornly through the valleys, routed by the fiery sun. Dust lay upon the spiny links and flaming blossoms of the cactus. The waters fled away, trailing a long skeleton of stones across the parching landscape. The wild doves beset the wasting pools, lamenting the eternal drought with their mournful cooing, and the red deer grew tamer than the cattle of the plains from very thirst. And so the summer days passed by; until September came, and with it the momentous trial at Oskaloo.

XV

THE site of the town of Oskaloo was largely responsible for the unfortunate reputation of its inhabitants. Its surroundings were malarial. The village lay in a low, marshy district, encircled on three sides by a stagnant stream. A damp, offensive, depressing mist crept in at evening to brood above its silent streets, and distribute fever and ague with a generous hand. The only avenue of escape from this plague-infested *cul-de-sac* was the trail road which led undeviatingly out of town to the prairies and hills beyond. It was, therefore, with a feeling of misgiving that the wary traveler descended it. A similar sentiment prompted sojourners in that "happy valley" to decorate trees and bowlders by the wayside with warning placards and inscriptions. "Sacred to the memory of Ayer's Pills" was the flying testimony of one unfortunate.

Perhaps it was in consequence of these depressing atmospheric conditions that stimulating beverages were appreciated at Oskaloo. It would seem that an impression existed that the visible population varied directly in proportion to the presence and availability of something to drink.

" There didn't seem to be enough citizens about
to justify an enterprisin' census clerk," Judge Natchez
had remarked to Sheriff Mosely, after a preliminary
visit. " Has there been an earthquake, or an epidemic, or what ? "

" I reckon not," Mosely rejoined, with a humorous twinkle of the eye, " but I'll allow, jedge, ye
didn't give the boys any encouragement. Now, ef
you'd a-thought to set out a pail of old rye and a tin
dipper on thet thar stump in front of the blacksmith's
shop, you'd ha' seen a constitooency, to onct, thet
would ha' gladdened yer eyes. It's my opinion," the
sheriff continued, in easy disparagement of his birth-
place, " thet's about the only way an accurate and
satisfyin' census of the poppylation of Oskaloo can be
took."

Although the particular stump in front of the
blacksmith's shop, referred to by Mr. Mosely, was vacant on the morning of the 5th of September, the
crowded condition of the main street justified the
suspicion that some similar attraction was in the
neighborhood. The additional fact that the temper
of the gathering was genial, strengthened this opinion.
When it is added that actual hilarity and mirth pre-
vailed in the vicinity of a certain saloon which Mr.
Buck Jerrold had recently made his headquarters, the
situation will not admit of further doubt.

The fact was, a phenomenon had occurred at Oskaloo. For the first time within the memory of the
oldest inhabitant, unlimited refreshment for the inner
man had been available to combat the ills of a long
and soul-subduing summer. It had been customary,
twice in every year, for local dealers to encourage

trade by a judicious display, in front of their shops, of the seductive legend, "Whisky Free in the Back Room." But the inducement was offered to the purchaser, and not gratuitously to the general public. Now, however, this generous hospitality was within the reach of all. With the arrival of Mr. Jerrold, a hogshead of spirits was immediately put on tap at the "Long Divide Tavern"—a facetious title, supposed to refer to the previous infrequency of drinks at that well-known hostelry—and immediate patronage invited. Need it be said that the response was prompt ? The luckless citizens, living face to face with bilious fever, and a complaint, popularly known as "dumb ager," rallied at the call as at the sound of a clarion.

Nor only in the town itself — the news spread like wild-fire, and seemed to appeal directly to a long-felt want in outlying camps. For several days a nondescript throng of horsemen and pedestrians poured into Oskaloo, cheerfully unmindful of the wayside warnings already noticed. Even "Peter the Hermit," an aged vagabond, who, in company with two mangy, yellow dogs, dwelt on a lonely divide outside the settlement, found something in the announcement that dispelled his asceticism. He was discovered that morning, stumping along pensively on his crutches in eager haste to the village. Eventually he turned up at the tavern, in company with his four-footed companions, and, by a course of grotesque but hearty dissipation, brought disgrace upon his brotherhood and the apparent contempt of his two dogs.

It was frankly announced by Mr. Jerrold—albeit without the knowledge of Henry Bruce—that the "flow of soul," thus inaugurated at Oskaloo, was en-

14

tirely at the expense of the prisoner at the bar. It
was even suggested that this generosity was a gratuitous tribute, on his part, to the esteem in which he held
the inhabitants. There was a transparency about this
statement, in view of the coming trial, which was
ingenuous and charming. Howbeit, the potency of
the tribute seemed to disarm criticism. A strong un-
dercurrent of sympathy was apparent in favor of the
prisoner. He was regarded in the light of a public
benefactor. When this opinion began to manifest
itself openly, the district attorney made an effort for
impartiality by attempting to impanel a jury, and
hold them aloof from the spirit of philanthropy which
was becoming epidemic. He was met by a singular
obstacle. Fully one half of the citizens of Oskaloo
volunteered their services as jurymen ! At this un-
heard-of proposition the legal gentleman permitted
matters to take their own course.

Mosely did not hesitate to contribute his quota to
the favorable opinion. This was by a graphic and
thrilling account of the trick performed by Bruce
with the "Smith and Wesson" revolver at the San
Marcus ball. To have heard the sheriff describe this
episode was worth a hard day's riding ; to have seen
the rapt attention and appreciation of his auditors, a
much longer journey. So far from prejudicing the
popular feeling toward Bruce in regard to the killing
of Foraker, it gave an impression of proficiency with
the pistol so remarkable as to amount almost to justi-
fication. It began to be believed that it would be
little short of a crime to deal harshly with one so
gifted. " Pulled thet ' barrel-catch ' slick and clean,
boys, and slung them cartridges right and left, so thet

Lem was nowhar !" Mr. Mosely repeated, illustrating the act by practical manipulation of the deceased horse-thief's weapon. An awe fell upon the company. It was apparent that a hero in difficulties, and not a man in jeopardy of his life, awaited the respectful consideration of the citizens of Oskaloo.

When, therefore, Phil Kernochan arrived, bringing with him Henry Bruce, Judge Natchez, and Colonel Hunt, who, with a few of his troops, had joined them in the interests of order and justice, there was a rush to see the prisoner, and something like a public demonstration attempted. Colonel Bill Furey, the prosecuting attorney, viewed this proceeding with ill-favor. He glanced appealingly at Judge Pemberton, who had dismounted from his buggy, and, leaning upon the wheel, was placidly smoking his cigar in conversation with the sheriff. The action recalled that worthy. He threw aside his cigar, and at once led the way to the court-house. With shouts and much scrambling for first positions, the disorderly crowd followed.

It was a hot day, and the little court-room was soon crowded to suffocation. Nevertheless, in spite of the discomfort of their surroundings, a singular levity and good humor possessed the audience. No sooner were the few chairs and benches exhausted, than the throng cheerfully availed themselves of the floor and window-sills of the court. Here, packed in on every side like sardines, they evinced the liveliest interest in the proceedings. A disposition was apparent to assist the lawyers in selecting the jury. As each man's name was called, he was greeted with cheers and cries of encouragement, and any reluctance to serve provoked a storm of opposition. Under these circumstances the preliminary business of the trial was not transacted without some delay and irritation on the part of judge and lawyers. By the time the jury were sworn, his Honor had worn himself out in his efforts to preserve order, and the audience had shouted itself hoarse in abuse and personalities. A feeling of exhaustion supervened. It was apparent that something must be done. When, therefore, the prisoner's counsel rose in his place to address the court, he received the attention of all present.

"Your Honor," said Judge Natchez, mopping his heated brow with a red bandanna handkerchief, and regarding the flushed features of the justice, who sat indignant, arbitrary, and collarless, at the head of the long table that answered for the judicial bench, "before proceeding to trial, I would state that the perliminaries of this case have been powerful tedious, and I submit that the gravity of the indictment necessitates that this court adjourn and take a drink."

There was a dead silence. All eyes were fastened upon the judge. Wherein the situation differed from a previous one, when he had withstood temptation thus directly offered, I can not say. Perhaps the stifling atmosphere may have been too much for his conscience; for, as a matter of fact, his Honor reached silently for his hat, and, drawing it over his eyes, started abruptly for the door. His example was followed. In precisely three minutes after this popular proposal of the prisoner's counsel, the court-room was vacant.

It appeared subsequently that, during this inter-

val, a singular rivalry was manifested between Mr.
Buck Jerrold and Judge Natchez, at the bar of the
"Long Divide." It was in the matter of fortifying
the jury against the eloquence of opposing counsel.
The solicitude of both parties was great, and the rivalry keen—so keen, in fact, that the "twelve good
men and true" grew mellow and philosophic under
treatment. Seeing which, Judge Pemberton felt
called upon at last to thump loudly on the bar with
his empty tumbler, and order a peremptory return to
the court-room. This being done, his Honor laid aside
his coat and vest, and, rising to his feet, addressed the
assembled court-room briefly.

"It appears," remarked Judge Pemberton, vaguely,
frowning darkly in evidence of the affront offered his
judicial dignity by recent events—"it appears, that a
disposition is on foot to defeat the ends of justice by
tamperin' with this yer jury. What I knows, I knows,
and seen myself. It hez got to be stopped, or I'll
impose fines here for contempt of court, thet'll bankrupt the hull county to pay 'em! Ez to how much
the counsel in this case, their friends, and the audience, gener'ly, feel called upon to hoist, in order to
grapple with the case in hand, I hev nothin' to say.
Thet's their bizness. But thet thar jury is mine, and
I propose to run them myself.—Sheriff Mosely, you
will quarantyne them twelve men durin' dinner, and
until they reach a vardict. I hold you pussonally
responsible for the mental condition of the hull caboodle."

This severe rebuke cast a temporary gloom over
the court-room, that his Honor's complicity in the
recent conviviality could not entirely subdue.

When, at length, the case of "The People *vs.* Henry Bruce" was formally opened, it appeared that the district attorney would "call the attention of the intelligent bench before him, to one of the most cruel and blood-curdling murders of modern times." The incredulity with which the jury received this announcement, was decidedly discouraging to the State's representative. It appeared, however, that this version of the case rested on the attorney's unsupported statement. There were no witnesses to the highly ingenious and thrilling assassination of Captain Foraker which he proceeded to set forth in detail. When he attempted to offer in evidence the testimony of the sergeant of Foraker's men, as to what Lemuel Wickson had told him of the affair through the windows of the jail, Judge Natchez promptly objected. In the language of the prisoner's counsel, "Whereas Lem Wickson was deceased, contrary to his own expectation, this fairy-tale of thet thar hoss-thief was no ante-mortem statement." Sheriff Mosely was sworn, and testified, moreover, that at the time of the affray between Foraker and the prisoner, Wickson was in close custody, and some three miles from both parties. "Pr'aps, boys," said Ike, winking craftily at certain of his fellow-townsmen, ranged on the jury benches, "you'll let thet pettyfoggin' old skeesicks delude you into the idee, that Lem hed the sight of a Mexican buzzard, and could spot the hull situation from thet thar distance!"

But, here, Judge Pemberton, whose judicial conscience was now thoroughly aroused, asked the sheriff on which side of the case he was retained, and called him sternly to order. Ike gravely descended from the stand, after assuring the jury that he was on the same side as his Honor and all lovers of law and justice.

It was then developed that all the evidence in the case rested upon the unsupported statement of Henry Bruce, who was sworn in his own defense. He was asked to give an account of the killing, which he did in a few direct and simple words. The sincerity of his manner, the dignity of his bearing, and the quiet manliness of Bruce in his trying position had its weight with his judges. But there was one fact which more than anything else compelled the reverence of this Lone Star tribunal. It was this : that the man who stood before them, on trial for his life, had been able to disarm an outlaw, in the act of brandishing a Smith and Wesson "six-shooter" at full cock ! It may be doubted whether, in view of the recent adjournment, certain of the jury were not in doubt as to whether this was not the real cause at issue. At any rate, the foreman permitted his features to relax in smiling scrutiny of the prisoner, during the taking of his testimony.

Nevertheless, it was with anxiety in his face and manner, that Mr. Buck Jerrold approached Sheriff Mosely when the court took a recess for dinner.

"What's up ?" inquired Ike, noting his companion's dejection. "I reckon the prevailin' opinion is favorable, Buck," he continued, glancing in at the open door of the tent, where the arbiters of the fate of Henry Bruce were serenely discussing their noonday meal.

"Thet's jest it !" replied Mr. Jerrold. "The opinion *is* favorable *now*, Ike, but sence you've got thet jury quarantyned, how long is it goin' to last ?

You must keep 'em up to it ! Ef I could only contrive to reach 'em with this universal pannyscer thet makes 'em so charitably disposed—well and good. I know the town, ye see, and it's gin'ral sentiments. When the reaction sets in, there's no holdin' 'em."

The gloom of Mr. Jerrold's manner gave the sheriff a sense of conviction. He became thoughtful at once. Suddenly his eye brightened. He drew himself up to the height of his small figure, and brought his right hand down with a vigorous slap upon the shoulder of Buck Jerrold. It seemed that all the nervous energy of his nature was concentrated in the two words he whispered—

"*Iced tea !*"

Closing one eye gravely upon the recipient of his information, he returned to an apparently watchful scrutiny of the twelve occupants of the boarding-tent.

In a surprisingly short space of time, a beverage, proffered under the above title, and bearing a strong resemblance, in color at least, to that familar metropolitan drink, began to circulate about the deal board and achieved instant popularity. If there was about this beverage a peculiar odor, entirely foreign to the national drink of China, it may have been owing to the fact that the large and substantial pitcher, in which it was dispensed, had subserved another purpose earlier in the day. Certainly the fact excited no comment from its patrons. But, when the jury left the social board, it was with no perceptible lowering of mien or manner, and it was even remarked that the easy roll, affected by some of them, was more in keep-

ing with the locomotion of the jolly Jack tar, than
the dilatory step which usually distinguishes the
Texan.

, I pass over the able and eloquent charge delivered
by Judge Pemberton, as not strictly necessary here.
Enough, that his Honor's exposition of the law was
made, with the assistance of certain notes and hiero-
glyphics, recorded with a piece of chalk on a pine
shingle, during the progress of the trial.   Enough,
that he emphasized his points, by carelessly tapping the bench with the handle of a Colt's "six-
shooter," which he had recently taken from his belt
to serve the purpose of the customary gavel.   Enough,
that, when he defined the law in accordance with a
certain state of facts, he staked his legal reputation
and a casual fifty dollars on the strength of his position.   Judge Pemberton did not direct a verdict,
though requested so to do by both Judge Natchez and
Colonel Furey, notwithstanding the fact that this was
a criminal action.   It was apparent that his Honor
desired to be just.   It was only when he dropped the
suggestion, that "frontier captains hed been givin' too
much lately to runnin' towns in Texas," that he was
supposed to betray his own personal convictions.   But
he retrieved this false step by an appeal for justice
that electrified the court-room.

Amid a breathless silence the jury left the benches
and repaired to the neighboring stable to deliberate
upon their verdict.   They were attended by a majority
of those present, who were stopped at the open door
of this building by the armed interposition of the
sheriff.   Nevertheless, some verbal advice was offered
them by the disappointed throng who could readily

discern their consulting figures, grouped about a dilapidated manger in the interior.

In the little court-room Judge Pemberton relaxed his dignity. He lighted a black clay pipe, tilted his chair back, and, stacking both his cowhide boots on a dilapidated law-book, clasped his hands behind his head in dreamy contemplation of the moldy ceiling. The prisoner and his counsel conversed in low tones. A sudden nasal murmur shook the court-room. The avenging spirit of Justice was beginning to nod.

There was a quick shuffling of feet at the doorway and a hurried rush for the court-room. The jury filed solemnly back. The prosecuting attorney entered hastily among the thronging citizens, suspiciously wiping his lips with his red bandanna. Judge Pemberton awoke with a prolonged snore, and, grasping his six-shooter, immediately rapped for silence, unfortunately in sleepy criticism of his own nasal efforts. Staggering hurriedly to his feet, he adjusted his glasses and frowned severely upon the serene and complacent twelve.

"Boys," said his Honor, gravely, "hev you agreed upon your vardict?"

"I reckon *so*, jedge," replied the foreman, with a broad grin.

"How say you? Is the prisoner guilty?"

"Guilty?" returned the foreman, with an incredulous sniff—"*not much!*"

"How hev you found, then?" inquired his Honor.

"Wal, jedge," the foreman responded, familiarly, while he leaned unsteadily on the legal table and comprehended the entire court-room in a single philanthropic smile—"ye see, it's about like this. We've sized the sitooation up and been over the whole bizness. Here's the diseased knows how peart the prisoner is with a six-shooter, and thet it's voluntary suicide to go ag'in him : accordin'ly, he gits bilin' full, and allows to lay him out ; natch'ally, diseased goes under ; and we finds prisoner *not guilty,* owin' to contribetary negligence on the part of diseased."

XVI.

THE elation of Phil Kernochan, over the result of the trial at Oskaloo, can be better imagined than described. In his triumphant joy the humor of the verdict was disregarded. He threw his arms about his partner's neck and embraced him in the presence of the crowded court-room. And a score of times, during the journey back to the "Mesquite Valley Ranch," he would spur his horse to his side and clap him on his shoulder, in the transport of his delight over his release.

Bruce received his acquittal with philosophic calmness. But, while justified in his own conscience from the outset, as to the necessity of his act, he had been manifestly moved by the popular feeling in his behalf. Especially was he grateful for the action of Sheriff Mosely and Buck Jerrold. Although, in no sense, a party to the method by which these gentlemen had felt it necessary to forestall a prejudiced community in his behalf, he was deeply indebted for the impulse which prompted it. He attempted to convey some idea of his feelings to the two men, but was met by an emphatic denial of obligation. Mr. Jerrold claimed that Bruce had conferred a personal favor upon him and the public at large, by the killing of the late Captain Foraker. The sheriff maintained, as stoutly, that it was only by the indulgence of the ranchman that he was alive at all, and that he was morally bound to act as he did.

It was a joyful return to the "Mesquite Valley Ranch." Difficult, indeed, would it be to exaggerate the enthusiastic welcome of the impulsive Kate ; the overjoyed, though restrained, greeting of the more conservative Edith ; for, in the brief interval of his absence, Miss Stafford had passed some very lonely hours, and had found time to realize how much the presence of Bruce had grown to be to her. If she had reflected with bitterness upon the change in his attitude toward her ; if she had found the contrast between Miss Dallas and herself so overwhelming that she almost pitied Bruce for the blindness of his own vision : there was nothing strange or unfeminine in all this. Indeed, considering the tender regard the lady entertained for the ranchman, it was quite natural that she should be convinced, that she was the one person in the wide world to make him happy. Quite as natural was it, that she should see nothing but misery for him in indulging this unexplainable regard for Miss Dallas ; that she should believe Bruce to be the victim of some species of enchantment ; and that the prestige of her own birth and position should inspire her with little but aversion and contempt for her rival.

Actuated by these feelings, the fair Edith, during the first hours of his return, laid aside the pique that she had shown of late, and displayed an arch and playful manner that Bruce had once found irresistible. It was the old Edith, whose nameless grace and charm had once well-nigh betrayed him into a declaration. For a time he appeared like one fascinated by a memory of the past, and Edith was about to congratulate herself upon the return of her influence, when one morning she beheld him saddle his horse and ride away, without taking leave of her as of old. It was three days before he again appeared at the "Mesquite Valley Ranch." Miss Stafford needed no prompting as to the nature of his journey. The direction in which his horse had been headed settled that. But she was grieved and indignant. Without stopping to trace the steps by which she arrived at this conclusion, she felt herself terribly outraged and wronged. She was vindictive in consequence. Howbeit, she resolved to make one more determined effort to regain her ascendency. She would, if possible, remove Bruce from the influence of this rural siren who was fast teaching him to forget the requirements of his rank of life. If in the interval Cynthia, finding herself abandoned, should decide to crown the hopes of one so suitable as the gloomy Mr. Jerrold, Miss Stafford would renew her childish belief that "all marriages were made in heaven."

In this strait, she appealed to Kernochan to fulfill a promise, given long before, to take them on a fortnight's trip to Austin, the capital of the State. She reminded him that her visit was drawing to a close, and that the time was short in which to keep his word. Her indulgent host readily acquiesced.

When this trip had been decided upon, Phil Kernochan proposed that the four should ride over to San Marcus on horseback, it being necessary that he and his partner should arrange some business matters before their departure. The proposal was received with favor.

Before setting out, Miss Stafford repaired to her room, where she arrayed herself in the faultless riding-dress with which she had once electrified Miss Dallas. As she peered into her toilet-mirror, there was a grim resolve about the lines of her mouth from which her quick-witted sex might have argued no quarter to a rival. And it was noticeable that the few additional hair-pins, with which the lady found it necessary to secure her raven tresses, were placed in position almost fiercely—very much as Miss Edith might have used a harpoon upon some creature that had excited her resentment. When her toilet was completed, she surveyed herself from head to foot critically, but with evident approval; after which she opened a small jewel-casket, and, taking from an inner recess a ring, she slipped it hurriedly upon the third finger of her left hand. It was a solitaire diamond, large and brilliant, and she passed her small handkerchief across it once or twice, catching the morning sunlight on the flashing jewel, and noting how it graced her dimpled hand. But there was an expression in the lady's dark eyes that was hardly reassuring.

The ring was a mere memory with Edith—a souvenir of an attachment from which the sentiment had long since faded—a relic of an almost forgotten past. Howbeit, although she usually wore no rings, she permitted it to remain upon her finger that morning, and, drawing her riding-glove quickly over the gem, she joined the mounted party at the ranch-gate, where the impatient Phil was calling loudly upon the ladies to hurry.

After dinner that afternoon, when Kernochan and
Bruce had left them to transact the inevitable business ; and Kate, weary with the morning's ride, had
insisted on taking a *siesta,* in spite of the stuffy atmosphere of the San Marcus Hotel ; Edith was dominated by a sudden energy. She leaned against a window of the dreary parlor, and gazed down the dusty
road toward the green foliage of the river. How cool
it looked there ! And what a short distance away !
What was to prevent her going there, if she would ?
She answered this question by ordering the sleepy
proprietor to have her pony saddled and brought to
the front gallery at once.

Having succeeded in gaining the saddle unassisted,
with an ease and dash that left that worthy speech-
less and staring, Miss Stafford rode quietly out of
town. When she reached the river, she did not stop,
but guiding her unwilling mustang skillfully across
the shallow ford, she turned in the shade of the trees
upon the opposite bank, taking the direction of the
Dallas Ranch. She knew its general position from a
remark of Bruce during the week of the San Marcus
Ball. She did not think the distance great. Hardly
had she taken the trail-road, when she encountered
Buck Jerrold, riding along listless and dejected upon
the gaunt " Buckshot."

The man raised his serious face and saluted her
gravely. Edith drew rein. Grateful for her rescue
some months previous, the fastidious Miss Stafford
treated him with uniform courtesy ; just now, the
meeting was most opportune. Did Mr. Jerrold know
the distance to the Dallas Ranch, and would he direct
her to it ? Buck stared, gave the information in the

usual blind Southern fashion, but did not volunteer
any personal guidance. Edith, moreover, did not request it. But was Miss Cynthia at home ? Mr. Jerrold
stared again, and reckoned she was. Miss Stafford
thanked him, and dashed away in the direction indicated, leaving the cow-man gazing solemnly after her.
But, as she rode, Edith reflected upon his gloomy
bearing, and was not without feeling that she was
acting very generously toward him, in the utterly
selfish purpose she had in mind.

Cynthia was in her bower, whither, of late, she had
been much given to repairing. She was lying in her
hammock, swinging listlessly to and fro, her half-
closed eyes dreamily regarding the ever-swaying curtain of green above her head. The flecked shadows
played over her face and red-gold hair, as the hammock swung, and, reckless of sun-tan or exposure,
she had thrown her arms above her head, her fingers
carelessly intertwined. "Aulus," graver and more
dignified than usual, crouched at her feet.

She was happy—happier than she had ever felt or
known before ; and as she swung there, her guardian
brothers of the wood seemed to nod and beckon, as if
in sympathy with the happiness she felt. For, had
not he, who had brought this new-found happiness
into her life, come forth unscathed from the troubles
and dangers surrounding him ? She recalled the weariness and anxiety of the previous days ; the fear with
which she had flown to her father and besought him
to take her to the trial in the distant frontier town,
that she might personally, by her presence and sympathy, sustain him in the hour of his distress. She
remembered the amazement and indignation of Al-

15

cides, who turned for relief, after this unblushing request of his fair daughter, to a frenzied rehearsal of his favorite symphony upon his violin.

But it was all over now. He was safe; he had returned; she was content. And yet, in the restful quiet of the little wood, Cynthia could not but feel a pang of pity for the man who had just left her with no hope in his eyes, to whose generous conduct much of the present joy she felt was due.

There was the sound of a footstep without, and the girl sprang to her feet with a sudden flush. She put both hands to her head as if to efface any disorder of her tresses due to her previous attitude. A broad shaft of sunlight, slipping through the branches overhead, steeped in glowing warmth her picturesque face and figure.

A moment of expectation, and Miss Stafford, cool, erect, and fastidious, holding her immaculate skirts in the gloved fingers of her right hand, stepped within. As she did so, she toyed carelessly with the riding-whip held in her left, and gazed curiously about her. Their eyes met. Miss Stafford bent her head coldly, and permitted Cynthia the slightest inclination of her arched eyebrows. The recognition of Miss Dallas was equally cordial.

An embarrassing pause followed these civilities. Edith was the first to break it.

" I suppose you are surprised to see me here," she began, with more embarrassment of manner than she had deemed possible. She glanced down at the whip she held lightly between her gloved fingers. Cynthia remained quiet.

" The fact is, Miss Dallas," Edith recommenced,

the hesitation of her manner lending an apparent sincerity to her words—"the fact is, I am going away very soon ; but I felt I could not do so, without thanking you for your kindness to me in being so good to Mr. Bruce."

Cynthia raised her eyebrows and stared blankly at Edith, turning her head a little one side—very much as a bird will, when doubtful if it has heard aright. She grew a shade paler, but replied that she was gratified, if anything she had done had found favor with Miss Stafford. If look and manner, however, counted for anything, it was quite evident that the temperature of Cynthia's gratification was indefinitely below zero.

"I mean by your riding over to his assistance in the reckless fashion you did," Miss Stafford continued. "It was really quite romantic and kind of you, you know—quite what one reads about ; and I wanted to—to thank you. I told Mr. Bruce so. I know he feels much as I do."

There was a very perceptible change in Cynthia's manner while listening to this ingenuous statement. Apparently she grew several inches taller under Miss Stafford's patronage. Her lip curled perceptibly and her eyes flashed, as she implied very decidedly that she was quite aware what Mr. Bruce thought about it.

"Very possibly," Miss Stafford assented, quietly— "but I was only telling you what he said to *me*. I am going away, you know—we are *both* going away." Miss Stafford emphasized the "both." "I thought you ought to know how we felt in the matter."

The ominous plural fell like a knell upon Cynthia. She felt her breath grow quick and short, and a sud-

den faintness seize her.   But she did not change her
attitude.   She remained gazing steadfastly up into
the beautiful face before her.   There was disdain in
the brown eyes, and she felt it.

"And so you turned yourself into Henry Bruce's
errand - boy to let me know," she replied, calmly.
"Well, now, thet's kind of you, I'm sure ; you reckoned I was just natch'ally lyin' awake nights to get
your approval, and you couldn't rest until you took
this way of showin' it.   P'raps you'll be willin' to
say, Miss Stafford, how long you've been carryin' his
messages and runnin' his errands ? "

She threw back her head and laughed merrily, as
she said this—a laugh so musical and clear that it
seemed to ripple upward from the very heart of joy.
Miss Stafford blushed crimson beneath her merriment.
It steeled her to adhere to her original purpose.   With
a sudden gesture she stripped off the glove upon her
left hand ; the glittering facets of the diamond she
wore flashed in the broad shaft of sunbeams that cleft
the bower.

"Do you see that ring ? " she demanded, coldly,
suffering the fascinated eyes of the girl to rest a moment upon the sparkling gem.   "Perhaps that will
explain my interest in the welfare of Mr. Bruce."

She turned proudly, flashed one brief glance of
triumph upon Cynthia from beneath her supercilious
lashes, and swept haughtily out of the bower.   Cynthia was alone with the agony of the sudden revelation.

She put one hand to her head in a half-dazed way,
as if she felt a sudden pain there.   The ground seemed
slipping away beneath her feet ; the horizon whirled

around her. She felt in one brief instant as if the sunlight had gone from the earth—the vivid blue from the sky; and the next she was lying prone upon the mosses at her feet, weighed down by the gray, despairing monotone that seemed suddenly to possess all things. She pressed her hands over her eyes, burying her face deep down in the soft lichens, as if to shut out of sight the dreadful reality which suddenly confronted her. Then a quick tremor shook her, and she was crying silently as if her heart would break.

How long she lay there, overcome by the weight of this sudden sorrow that had come into her life, Cynthia did not know. She was only aware, in an indefinite way, that the chirp of cricket and grasshopper throbbed monotonously through the consciousness of her woe; that the birds seemed to sing carelessly as if in mockery of it; and that through it all her faithful " Aulus " fawned about her with rude caresses and strove to comfort her.

And so he was really engaged to Miss Stafford; that was the end, then. This man whom she had so trusted and believed had been playing a double part with her, and had called her out of the ignorant content of her early life, only to crush her with the new joy he had awakened. Oh, the pity of it! And she had shown she loved him so ! Overcome by the bitterness of this reflection, she sank down again, and lay there pale and wretched, twining her fingers listlessly in the soft mosses, her eyes fixed on vacancy, and oblivious of all else, save this one, mortifying, humiliating, agonizing fact.

The moments went slowly by. The shadows shifted

on the pine-strewn floor.   High overhead a squirrel,
that had marked her grief, dropped a cone down upon
her as if in protest.   A motionless red lizard, that at
first seemed to sympathize with her, leered at her
from an adjacent stone, and was growing visibly hys-
terical.   And then this irony of Nature was dispelled
by a footstep that came quickly into the bower.   The
squirrel flashed suddenly around a limb, and the lizard rustled off into the thicket.   Cynthia raised her
eyes.   Henry Bruce was standing over her, regarding
her with a curious, questioning glance.

She gave him no word or sign of recognition.   The
one brief glance with which she swept his face had in
it the scorn and contempt of the injured woman.
She sprang to her feet, dashing away from her, with a
passionate gesture, the hand he had extended to her
aid.   Turning her back upon him, she sought the
farthest corner of the bower.

Bruce was astounded at this reception.   He took
a step or two toward her and attempted to take her
hands in his.   She whipped them indignantly behind
her and faced him with flashing eyes.   In his ignorance of what had passed, the young ranchman cast
about him for some act of his that could have caused
this sudden anger.

"Cynthia," he said, breaking the silence, "what
is the meaning of this ?   I am going away on a brief
trip to Austin.   I have come to bid you good-by.
Have you no word to say to me ? "

She waved him away with an imperious gesture.

"There is no need of it," she said.   "I have received your good-bys already, from *her !* "

Bruce stared.   He gave a surprised glance about

him. Lying at his feet among the pine-needles was a
dainty glove of undressed kid. He recognized it
instantly as belonging to Edith. Involuntarily he
stooped and picked up the perfumed trifle. It was
redolent of its owner. He turned with a look of inquiry to Cynthia.

"Has Miss Stafford been here ?" he asked, almost
sternly. He was hardly prepared for the icy brevity
of her reply :

"Yes."

"And she told you I was going away ?"

"She said you were *both* going," said Cynthia,
simply. The word seemed to choke her, but she recovered herself with an effort. "She showed me the
ring that you gave her, and said she wished to thank
me for my kindness to you."

In spite of herself, the tears started to the girl's
beautiful eyes. An angry flush came suddenly over
the face of Bruce.

"It is strange that, as one personally interested, I
learn of this now for the first," he said, dryly. "Am
I to understand that Miss Stafford told you I gave her
a ring ?"

"She gave me to understand that she was engaged
to you," said Cynthia, quickly, looking him straight
in the eyes.

Bruce took a step nearer to her.

"It is false !" he said, with white lips.

A sudden revulsion of feeling crimsoned Cynthia's
face and neck. She regarded him earnestly.

"False ?" she whispered.

Bruce took the little brown hands in his, and
looked down into her face.

"False !" he said. "Don't you know, darling, there is but one girl in the wide world I would be willing to make my wife ?"

She looked up at him shyly through the tears of a moment before.

" Who is thet ?" sne said.

" Cynthia Dallas ! "

THE END.

www.ingramcontent.com/pod-product-compliance
Lightning Source LLC
Chambersburg PA
CBHW030107030726
47498CB00007B/2282